WAR OF THE WORLDS

THE ANGLO-MARTIAN WAR, 1895

BY MIKE BRUNTON

ILLUSTRATIONS BY ALAN LATHWELL

First published in Great Britain in 2015 by Osprey Publishing,
PO Box 883, Oxford, OX1 9PL, UK
PO Box 3985, New York, NY 10185-3985, USA
Email: info@ospreypublishing.com

Osprey Publishing is of part Bloomsbury Plc.

A CIP catalog record for this book is available from the British Library

Print ISBN: 978 1 4728 1156 1
PDF e-book ISBN: 978 1 4728 1157 8
EPUB e-book ISBN: 978 1 4728 1158 5

Typeset in Garamond Pro, Verve and Conduit ITC
Originated by PDQ Media, Bungay, UK
Printed in China through Worldprint Ltd.

15 16 17 18 19   10 9 8 7 6 5 4 3 2 1

Osprey Publishing is supporting the Woodland Trust, the UK's leading woodland conservation charity, by funding the dedication of trees.

www.ospreypublishing.com

"For Alison, Thomas and Matt, who were kind enough to believe in Martians."
–MB

CONTENTS

CHAPTER 1
INTRODUCTION

In 1895 the United Kingdom of Great Britain and Ireland was, as far as its ruling classes were concerned, experiencing a golden age of prosperity and peace. Lawn tennis, an afternoon of cricket on the village green, and the prospect of a peaceful, British century ahead were the only things that concerned people in August 1895. It was clear to everyone who mattered (and quite a few foreigners) that God was definitely an Englishman, and that was that. The business of running the world, and remaining a gentleman while doing so, was quite enough for Queen-Empress Victoria's loyal subjects.

Englishmen – using the term loosely, as the Victorians did, to mean 'Britons' and include Scots and Welshmen – had won life's lottery. Many felt they had a mission to bring the benefits of Christian order and civilization, which was to say British order and civilization, to all corners of the world. One-fifth of the world's population lived within the Empire; more would surely welcome the prospect. The Royal Navy furthered this aim by acting as the world's policeman, maintaining the Pax Britannica, a peace at once benign and in Britain's interests. The British Army served across the Empire to fight rebels and malcontents at the margins. Steady, stately progress towards a better tomorrow was guaranteed.

Herbert George Wells, 1866–1946, was the most evocative of the war correspondents but not the most accurate. The plight of the common man inspired his work, and he was later criticized as unpatriotic and even 'pro-Martian' for his view that the Martians were unbeatable.

This rosy, slightly smug picture was illusory. Britain's industries had been overtaken by both America and Germany; many of the colonies actually drained resources from Britain rather than provided wealth; serious resentments simmered below the surface in places like South Africa; and international tensions with other Powers were growing, as other nations built their own empires. But the crisis of August 1895 was not one of Britain's making, or a result of foreign machinations.

The 'War of the Worlds', the 'Martian Invasion' or the 'First Anglo-Martian War' (this last name giving rise to a dread that there would be a second war) was different to all other wars fought by the British. The attack came out of nowhere: there were no dark clouds on the political horizon to act as a warning to Victoria's ministers. The Martians fell, literally, out of a clear blue sky. And in the space of 15 days they made the Home Counties and London a battleground more deadly than any British soldiers had ever faced. It was an unexpectedly short war for the existence of Britain, the Empire and, ultimately, humanity itself. That it ended as it did, in the defeat of the Martians, owed more to whimsical chance than grand strategy and bravery on the battlefield, although there was courage aplenty.

This is a history of that short, cruel and genocidal war, reconstructed from the perspective of the surviving human defenders. Like all such histories, it has inaccuracies and omissions. Some incidents can only be reconstructed from partial and incomplete accounts: among the British there were few survivors of battles against the Martians, and even fewer who had any wish to remember and recount their experiences. Other accounts were suppressed (destroyed in all probability) by the government in the interests of public morale and Imperial security. The physical evidence and documentation vanished into government archives, protected by the civil service's love of secrecy.

There are no Martian accounts or documents of any kind about the Invasion. Not a single recognizable account or record was ever recovered from the Cylinders or the Martians' remarkable machines. Their true motives, thoughts and intentions remain as much a mystery today as they were when they fell from the heavens. It has been possible to reconstruct a plausible explanation (to a human, at any rate) for what occurred, but much is speculative. Until human explorers penetrate the caverns of Mars, and read whatever Martian records might be found there, no account will ever be wholly accurate.

This, then, is an account of Britain's first, and so far only, interplanetary war. It was unlike any war fought before, the two sides so mismatched that the outcome should never have been in doubt. For once, the tide of history ran in a different direction, which is why this book is not written in the Martian tongue. It is a history written by the vanquished, not the victors.

CHAPTER 2
FORCES AT WAR

THE BRITISH

> If we are to *maintain* our position as a *first-rate* Power we must, with our Indian empire and large Colonies, be *Prepared for attacks* and *wars, somewhere* or *other*, CONTINUALLY.
>
> *Queen Victoria, letter to Gladstone (quirky emphases in the original).*

In the summer of 1895, as the Martian Cylinders fell, a British general election had just ended. Lord Salisbury's Conservatives had returned to power in alliance with the Liberal Unionists (those Liberals who did not favour Home Rule for Ireland). With 411 seats Salisbury's men handily defeated Lord Roseberry's Liberals and were, as might be expected, broadly isolationist, socially conservative, believers in the Empire, and vehemently opposed to Irish Home Rule. The Tories had managed to bring down Roseberry's government by claiming that the Liberals were failing to ensure enough cordite for ammunition for both the army and navy. The new administration was to be a steady hand on the national tiller, and highly unlikely to do anything radical. They would need every ounce of cordite they could get...

Robert Gascoyne-Cecil, Third Marquess of Salisbury, was a direct descendant of William Cecil, Lord Burleigh, a minister of no small ability for Elizabeth I. Politics were the marrow of Salisbury's bones, and he was deeply hostile to any form of 'state socialism', which to him meant doing anything to improve the lot of common folk, or any change in the established political order. It was his job to maintain Britain and the ordered life of its honest folk, as well as preserve the position and privileges of the aristocracy. He would have no truck with anything that smacked of change, fundamental or otherwise. As the prime minister, he found a threat to his beloved country greater than the Spanish Armada in the days of his illustrious ancestor Lord Burleigh.

Once the first Cylinders landed, Salisbury's government faced problems almost beyond their ken. They were suddenly thrust into the situation of a spear-armed African native facing European machine guns for the first time. That this was pointed out to them by experienced officers was not welcome. It was a deeply uncomfortable thought and one that Salisbury could not accept.

If Salisbury felt overwhelmed by the Martians he gave no outward sign but, aged 65, he was profoundly shocked. To see England's 'Splendid Isolation' cruelly violated was almost more than he could bear. Yet bear it he did, rallied himself and took three swift decisions: to remove all the

Royal Family to Balmoral Castle in Aberdeenshire, there to be guarded by an infantry battalion and whatever artillery batteries were nearby; to place London and the Home Counties under martial law with Sussex, Hampshire and possibly Kent alerted to expect the same; and to evacuate the government from London when practicable and without too much fanfare. He also decided that the Prince of Wales, who was enjoying one of his many holidays, would be separately kept out of harm's way; he would be allowed to go grouse shooting on 12 August as planned, but only if he went to a Scottish estate. The Cabinet then argued about the troops to guard Her Majesty: the sensible solution would have been to assign men from a Scottish garrison. Incredibly, ministers were worried about offending Her Majesty's dignity (as if Martians tramping around Surrey were not offence enough!) by using a line battalion. In the end the 1st Battalion, Grenadier Guards were sent to Scotland by chartered express.

An air of unreality hung over many government meetings during the crisis. Time was spent agreeing that 'un-English behaviour' in the face of the Martians would not be tolerated, and texts warning of the 'serious consequences of collaborating' with the invaders were drafted and approved. The consequences were never clearly spelled out, even within government circles, and this allowed legal justification for the later excesses of the military and the police. Newspaper space was booked so that announcements could be printed. Of course, no-one in government knew that collaboration would lead, inevitably, to death by exsanguination in the Martian camps. However, this emergency order served as the basis for actions against looters and malcontents in the East End of London. Meanwhile Salisbury's ministers made no evacuation arrangements for the ordinary people of London: that would have been 'state socialism'. Fortunately, better-off Londoners escaped by using the railways, but otherwise they were on their own. The emergency warnings and decrees appeared in the morning newspapers on Monday 12 August 1895. As they read the morning papers, Britons began to worry.

Lord Salisbury, the new Tory prime minister in summer 1895. He wisely left the detailed direction of the war to his generals, but he also left many Britons to look after themselves during the crisis. It was not, in his view, the job of government to help people who would not help themselves.

THE BRITISH ARMY

Victoria's army was not a typical European force except for its rather smart uniforms and slightly archaic weaponry. It was not ready, or large enough, to fight a European war.

It was there to protect and police the Empire against native threats as it was a matter of geography that Britain's defence was a naval matter; the army would defend its home only in direst need.

The British Army was an all-volunteer force, not conscripted, although undoubtedly some volunteers joined up as an alternative to prison or penury. It was, like British society itself, sometimes damaged by distinctions of class, resistant to many new ideas and, on occasion, horribly misused by politicians. It was also the poor relation: the Royal Navy took the lion's share of defence spending, and generated the lion's share of national pride to match. Generals had good reason to feel slightly resentful at their place in the queue for resources. Despite these issues it was a fairly good army at the battalion and regimental levels. Small wars across the Empire had produced an effective fighting force, but not a large one.

The British Army, at heart a conservative institution, was still coming to terms with reforms brought in after the Indian Mutiny and Crimean War. The Crimea in particular had been a shock, because the British public finally got timely reports on the war, the mistakes made, and the generals in command. Shortly afterwards, the Indian Mutiny had brought the East India Company's European regiments under government control. Both of these events, and the needs of the Empire, meant that soldiering was no longer all about perfect turnout for parade, but also about fighting skills. Over the following decades, the need to keep large numbers of British troops in India made the whole army more 'Indian' in terms of experience and outlook. Even the language and slang used by soldiers were changed.

Edward Cardwell, the Secretary of State for War under Gladstone in the early 1870s, brought major changes to the way the British Army was manned and organized. Cardwell was impressed by Prussian achievements during the Franco-Prussian War, and wanted the same professional rigour for the British Army. Service conditions improved, with flogging and similarly harsh punishments ended. He did away with 21-year terms of service and introduced a shorter term, but added time in the reserves after active duty; this was to build up a large number of men with military experience. Cardwell couldn't create a conscript army like the Prussians, so he did the next best thing.

The other big change in Cardwell's reorganization was to link regiments to specific locales. Before Cardwell, the whole country had been one big recruiting area for every regiment; after him, units recruited in their assigned areas. This made sense for the reserve system too, as men could be expected to return to their home counties and live in the vicinity of their old, local regiments. Local recruiting didn't happen immediately, but this kind of territorial connection was a good idea.

Ending the sale of commissions was the worst of all Cardwell's reforms for officers, because it hit them hard in monetary terms. Officers had always been able to buy their way into a regimental rank, or sell out if their regiment was posted to some unfashionable, inhospitable or disease-ridden spot. Wellington benefited from the purchase system: he bought his colonelcy, and that allowed him to become a relatively young field marshal by the time he won at Waterloo. The system was open to abuse, and always had been: men with money trumped men with military talent in getting commands. The best thing about commission purchase was that it gave an officer a lump sum on his retirement. If he had been lucky and not bought every promotion, or was in a reasonably fashionable regiment, an officer might make a tidy sum by selling on his commission at retirement.

As might be expected, many senior officers opposed Cardwell at every turn. Change was bad enough, but change on this scale was awful. Wasn't the old army good enough for Wellington and Marlborough? Although Cardwell left office in 1874, the anti-reformers

Prince George, Duke of Cambridge, the military head of the British Army, depicted in a typically patriotic pose of the period. Cambridge was an able administrator, but not a man comfortable with radical ideas. To his credit, he appointed an able man as field commander and gave his troops all the support he could. The strain of the Invasion contributed to his decision to retire shortly after the Martians' defeat.

did not manage to turn back the clock, and further reforms were introduced by Hugh Childers in 1881. Childers further reorganized infantry into multi-battalion regiments, complete with associated militia and volunteer battalions tied to particular depots and counties. This simple change did away with regimental seniority numbers (much to the annoyance of the senior, low-numbered regiments), and substituted district names.

While 20 years might seem like a long time, the senior officers in 1895 had grown up under the old system and then had the new foisted on them. The professional head of the army was a man who did not like reform or, in military matters at least, the unconventional. Prince George, the Duke of Cambridge and a cousin of Queen Victoria, had become commander-in-chief (the title changed over the decades he held it) in 1856, shortly after the Crimean War. He had been a cavalryman, and creditably led the 1st Division in the Crimea; he was a safe, conservative pair of hands to run the army. He became a fixture in Horse Guards, thanks to his close ties to Victoria. She had a proprietorial interest in her army, and was decidedly snobbish about its officer class. Cambridge suited the Queen perfectly: social status counted more than talent for command in his view. The Duke wanted 'reliable' officers drawn from the best and wealthiest families, people who could be relied on to maintain order at home and in the Empire. The aristocracy and landed gentry could be as brave as lions or as dangerously stupid as overbred spaniels, and were not always blessed with tactical or strategic genius. That Cambridge loved soldiering was never in doubt. To his credit, he had been responsible for establishing a staff college at Camberley, a good start towards improving professional standards and skills. And his personal life was anything but conservative: he had married his mistress for love, so falling foul of the 1772 Royal Marriages Act, which meant that his children could not inherit his titles or be in line to the throne.

The question of command on the ground could have been problematic. The Duke of Cambridge was not energetic enough to be a commander in the field. He, however, showed his true worth in suggesting another officer. General Lord Frederick Roberts was an extremely able man who would have risen to prominence in any army of the period. Roberts, recently returned from India and about to go to Ireland as commander-in-chief, was quickly given the job of driving out the Martians. He was under few illusions that this was going to be an easy task, but he was experienced, tough-minded and personally brave (as a lieutenant, he had been awarded a Victoria Cross for his gallantry during the Indian Mutiny). He was not a man to use dash and bravado instead of thought. He was an artilleryman, and had an appreciation of the power of machinery, something that was to serve him well against the Martians. By Monday morning of the first week, Roberts was hard at work, studying maps and reports of the Martians. He was explicitly ordered not to get himself killed, and to leave acts of conspicuous gallantry to younger men.

At regimental level professionalism was often seen as unsporting and, even worse, slightly un-British. A good polo player was more likely to be prized by his colonel than a supply or musketry expert. Officers who were 'too keen' or not quite 'one of us' could find their careers going nowhere through no real fault of their own. The system prized 'being a sound chap' and used quiet words in the right ears to promote the right kind of fellows. A sound chap from a good family who didn't funk under fire was assured of his place; the same was not true for the professional (which usually meant someone without the income a good family could supply).

Despite potential problems with officers, the rank and file of the British Army were usually tough and competent. 'Thomas Atkins', the average soldier, was well trained, and had equipment no worse than his fellows in other European armies. He had also seen action in every corner of the world. Tommy's weapons skills were very good, thanks to battlefield experience and the attention given to 'musketry' as it was archaically called. Equal time was given to bayonet drill because the bayonet was known to be the decisive weapon in the hands of steady, reliable troops. Reliability came from regimental tradition: every regiment taught every soldier to believe in its myths of dogged determination, courage and inevitable victory. Tommy Atkins did not ever cut and run in action: he would stand and fight, and as often as not win, against ridiculous odds, in almost impossible circumstances, in the most hostile of climates. It was, of course, these beliefs that allowed gentleman-amateur officers to throw away lives by careless leadership and still gain victory.

So, while the individual Tommy had shown excellent fighting qualities he was sometimes, too often perhaps, let down by the army's leadership. British troops fought well; British commanders came to rely on this, rather than their own skill, to win their wars. British generals were usually brave, patriotic and honourable, but this did not always make them great or useful commanders. The worst of them could be bull-headed, self-centred and ignorant of military realities, but fortunately Lord Roberts was far from being the worst.

Lord Frederick Sleigh Roberts had been recently promoted to field marshal and was expected to be the new Commander-in-Chief in Ireland. A brave and resourceful soldier, he was ordered to oppose the Martians with everything in England. By the middle of the first week, Roberts had few illusions about his chances of success but was determined to go down fighting.

His command comprised everything to hand in the Southern English garrisons. Home defence was one of the lesser tasks of the regulars in Aldershot, the main one being getting ready for postings overseas. The militia and volunteer battalions and Yeomanry cavalry were responsible for defence of the home islands. In effect, these part-time forces protected their own homes. When the call went out to confront the Martians, it turned out that they were not too keen on defending other people's homes. The regiments and battalions went, as duty demanded, but with no little grumbling and gaps in the ranks. Far too many men found reasons to stay at home and look to the defence of their own families and property. Both Cambridge and Lord Salisbury were frustrated at what Salisbury called '… this sad want of patriotism, of backbone, of manly British spirit…' Later, Salisbury saw to it that nothing was done to punish the reluctance of some part-timers. He saw no political gain in punishing men who were probably Tory or Unionist supporters.

As soon as it was clear that the Martians were hostile, the Duke of Cambridge realized it made no sense to recall overseas troops. The Martians could (perhaps would) be in London before any reinforcements arrived. Weakening colonial garrisons might embolden natives or, worse, encourage European nations into foolish adventurism.

Field days at Aldershot demonstrated the 'dash and fire' of the British Army in 1895, even as such ideas became suicidal on the battlefield. The army was an excellent force for fighting colonial wars, but not ready for a European conflict. The Martian War would test the army's mettle to breaking point.

Cambridge briefly considered using the Dublin garrison, but then rejected the notion as a risk to good order in Ireland. In this, Cambridge misjudged Irish sentiment. There was anti-British feeling but the Martians were seen as a greater threat, thanks to a widely reported sermon by Cardinal Michael Logue, the Archbishop of Armagh. On the Sunday after the landing, he denounced the Martians as servants of Satan. It was, he argued, a Catholic duty to make common cause against the ungodly aliens, and not use the crisis to weaken human (and that included English) strength. The 2nd Royal Irish and the 1st Royal Munster Fusiliers volunteered for service in Surrey immediately. They were ordered instead to organize anti-Martian watches in Ireland.

Sensibly, Cambridge saw that the army could only fight with those units already in the south-east. Any northern or Scottish forces would be needed if there were further landings. Within hours of the Woking landing, Cambridge's headquarters staff at Horse Guards sent alerts to the Aldershot Division, organizing the forces there into two infantry brigades and one (oversized) cavalry brigade. The gunners at Woolwich and sappers at Chatham were also warned of a move.

Aldershot was the home of the British Army in 1895. The brains might be at Horse Guards in London, the guns at Woolwich and the sappers on the Kent coast, but the guts of the army were in Aldershot, to the south-west of London. Aldershot was a military town and there was land for barracks, stables, field exercises, route marches, polo fields and everything else the army needed. It was also near enough to London for officers and men to enjoy all the capital's diversions. Sadly, among the lower ranks 'the Demon Drink' and boredom did their work every week, although keeping the men busy could do wonders. Among the officers things were sometimes no better: two officers were bullied (no other word is strong enough) out of the 4th Hussars simply because they lacked the income necessary to maintain the regiment's exclusive social standards. Mischief was the result if people were not kept busy.

A posting at Aldershot, busy or not, was actually something of a mixed blessing. Officers received very generous leave, and there was plenty of honest English beer for the men. There was no danger of sudden death at the hands of ungrateful locals, unlike some postings in the Empire. But what could have been a relatively staid life in barracks with sundry benefits on the side was disrupted: Aldershot was a little too close to Horse Guards. It was a convenient destination for senior officers bored with office life. Few of these gentlemen were able to resist the temptation of a comfortable train journey and a good dinner in one or other of the many regimental messes. This meant that a regiment so honoured also revelled in snap inspections, or had the pleasure of an (almost-impromptu) field day on Laffan's Plain, regardless of the weather. Inspections could be disruptive enough, but the field days – mock battles and practice manoeuvres – made uniforms and kit dirty, something that sergeants could not abide! And there was nearly always a march past at the end of the day, where any mistake would attract the sergeants' wrath upon the miscreants responsible. Generals' visits meant extra duties, and no sensible soldier ever welcomed extra duty.

Importantly for what was to come, most units stationed at Aldershot were under strength. It was quite usual for units to be as much as 40 per cent under their nominal manpower. It simply wasn't policy to keep more soldiers available than was strictly necessary. A unit brought itself up to numerical strength when it was preparing for an overseas deployment, or there was a war to be fought. The expeditionary nature of most of Britain's wars in the Victorian period meant that this had never been a problem. Wars were always carefully considered if they involved troops from Britain; it took weeks or months to organize and dispatch a force to fight in some far flung corner of the Empire. Fear of invasion had never entered these calculations either, because the Royal Navy would destroy any invaders before they set foot on English soil.

This lack of preparedness hurt the army when the Martians arrived: Aldershot's garrison was able to react swiftly to events, but not with huge numbers of men. Wars just didn't happen overnight, and they certainly didn't happen overnight in England! It could take days to summon a regiment's officers back to the colours and organize their baggage. Fortunately, the rank and file in barracks were a little more prepared for action, but under strength. This explains why the British Army went to war against the Martians in piecemeal fashion: in its homeland it could do little else.

The army did have plenty of equipment, most of it quite good. The weapons were all serviceable and proven in action. There were, however, shortages of ammunition. The 1895 General Election had been triggered by a scandal concerning cordite production and stocks, but Lord Salisbury took no comfort from being proved right on the issue.

The Lee–Metford was the standard rifle issued to regular infantrymen (some militia still had the older Martini-Henry). Introduced in the 1880s, this magazine rifle fired a .303 bullet, a smaller round than earlier weapons. The action, magazine and bolt had been designed by James Lee, while the barrel was the work of William Metford. The same rugged 'Lee' element was re-used to make the Short Magazine Lee–Enfield (SMLE) rifle which replaced the Lee–Metford shortly after the Invasion and stayed in service for the next 60 years. The Lee–Metford was supposed to use smokeless powder – cordite – cartridges, but older gunpowder cartridges were still being issued from stores. Gunpowder generates huge clouds of white smoke when fired: any unit using gunpowder cartridges immediately gave its position away, and the Martians quickly learned to target smoke clouds with Heat Rays. Firing at the Martians therefore became a death sentence for too many brave troops. The Lee–Metford itself was accurate, although incapable of damaging a Martian War Machine unless the shooter was uncommonly lucky and struck a viewing port. Even then, a penetrating shot was not a certainty, but crystalline fragments could and did cause wounds.

A carbine version existed for the cavalry. Despite boasting romantic regimental titles like hussars and lancers, British cavalry were equipped to fight as mounted infantry. Although nobody admitted it the days of the cavalry charge were long gone, even in 1895…

Officers were responsible for providing their own side arms, and had a free choice as long as the gun chosen used the standard .455 cartridges. Most chose the rugged and reliable Webley revolver. This was a handy weapon in close combat, but completely useless against the Martians. Oddly, for the first few days of the struggle, the Martians didn't bother searching captives. Churchill was able to hide his gun when he was captured, and dead officer

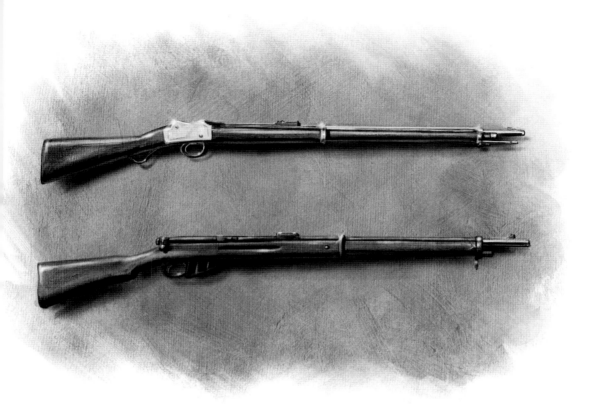

captives were found at landing sites with revolvers still in their possession.

The British Army had adopted the Maxim machine gun, largely at the insistence of General Sir Garnet Wolseley. He had ordered 120 Maxims in the late 1880s, chambered for the .577 bullets used by the Martini-Henry rifle. However, most of these were in the colonies and most officers, even if they thought about technical matters like Maxims, considered that they were suitable for use only against 'savages'. The few Maxims in Britain did not see action, because no one could think how to use them against the Martians until it was too late. As the final Martian Cylinders arrived suggestions were made to use the small number of Maxims available to saturate the crater around newly landed Cylinders with bullets, killing any emerging Martians before they could use their War Machines. This perfectly sensible idea was never put into practice.

The 'proper' artillery did have some very large cannons in forts guarding the Royal Navy's bases, such as the line of defences around Portsmouth. The weapons included 64-pounder rifled muzzle-loaders and 7in breech-loaders; a hit from any fortification gun could smash a War Machine to very small pieces as was shown at Shoeburyness on the Thames Estuary. But these guns were in emplacements, and unless a War Machine came into range, they were useless. Field artillery was all that could counter the invaders in a practical way.

Martini-Enfield and Lee-Metford rifles: the Lee-Metford was standard issue to British infantry and cavalry (in carbine form). The older Martini was issued to police forces and militia battalions. Both were largely useless against Fighting Machines but nothing else was available.

There were three types in England: two versions of the breech-loading 12-pounder and a slightly modified 15-pounder which actually fired a 14-pound (6.35kg) shell, just to be confusing – and all fired a 3in (76.2mm) shell. They also all used the same system of separate propellant charges and shells; a 15-pounder could fire 12-pounder shells at a pinch. All three were pulled by teams of six horses.

The seven-hundredweight (7cwt) 12-pounder was the oldest design, and was gradually being replaced. It hadn't proven reliable in the dusty conditions in India, and was considered too heavy for the horse artillery to keep up with cavalry. The simpler six-hundredweight (6cwt) gun had a shorter barrel and a better carriage, and was a more practical weapon. It used the same ammunition and, thanks to the arrival of cordite (although in limited amounts), it was in no way inferior to its heavier sibling.

The 15-pounder was a redesign that took advantage of cordite to fire a longer, heavier shell from an identical calibre of barrel. It was a heavier gun, of course, but its increased killing power more than made up for that.

All three guns were adequate for fighting terrestrial opponents. Against the Martians, it was crew quality and bravery that counted: a fast crew stood a chance of getting off enough rounds to give the Martians pause, even if they didn't destroy them. A slow or irresolute crew were usually cooked by a Heat Ray after their first shot.

THE ROYAL NAVY

In terms of fighting ability the Royal Navy was almost certainly the equal of all the other Great Powers' navies combined. Since Nelson's victory at Trafalgar in 1805 the Admiralty had maintained Britain's pre-eminent naval position regardless of cost. Steam power, ironclads and new-fangled weaponry had been quickly and efficiently adopted. Despite occasional flurries of excitement over foreign navies, the Royal Navy had kept its lead.

The navy was Britain's first, main and last line of defence, and it was inconceivable that enemies would set foot on British soil while it existed. The navy never went short of manpower, ships or money: it was a very courageous politician who even hinted the navy should get less funding. The admirals, though, must have felt they were on short rations simply because they were expected to defend all of the Empire and police the High Seas. The Royal Navy could legitimately claim that nothing moved at sea without Britain's approval, sometimes much to the annoyance of the other Great Powers. The navy could also claim that a latter-day Armada would have a very rough passage indeed while there were hardy Jack Tars at sea. It might – just might – be a job for the army, or possibly Scotland Yard, to round up the invaders who survived a salvo from the fleet.

Britons did get a taste of invasion from time to time, but only in the London weekly magazines. Fictional and untrustworthy foreigners visited all kinds of swinish, despicable cruelties on the inhabitants of the Home Counties before they were defeated by British pluck, manly honesty and cold steel. As events were shortly to prove, honesty, pluck and cold steel (British or otherwise) were of precious little use against a Martian Heat Ray.

Quite what the navy was to do against the Martians during the Invasion was never clearly set out by anyone: the Martians were plainly not sailors, and their landing grounds were far inland. In the end the navy did its share but it was not as a result of any grand strategy for defeating the Martians. Individuals found ways to attack the invaders.

The Admiralty did make sure that other European states could not interfere in the affair, and no foreign troops landed on English soil during or after the crisis. The navy also showed the flag across the Empire, even as London was besieged. The Royal Navy had always been a powerful symbol that the British Empire was more than Britain; now it was a symbol that the Empire would survive. Whether the navy could have maintained this fiction if all of England had been laid waste is doubtful, but this was never tested.

Admiral Sir John 'Jackie' Fisher, Third Sea Lord at the time of the Martians' arrival and the man who arranged to have London shelled by the Royal Navy. Fisher was ruthless, unbothered by collateral damage to civilian property, and wanted the Martians destroyed at all costs.

Their Lordships moved quickly to ensure the fleet was preserved. Portsmouth and Chatham were emptied of ships as quickly as possible, and by the Wednesday of the first week nothing significant was in harbour. At Portsmouth HMS *Majestic*, the largest battleship of her day, was being fitted out. By heroic efforts, she was towed out to sea, towards the Harland and Wolff shipyards in Belfast. Guns and other unfitted components were lashed to her decks and irreplaceable fitters, armourers and craftsmen were half-willing passengers. Such workers' families as could be gathered were quickly put aboard three steamers and sent after the *Majestic* convoy: the Admiralty was not staffed by heartless men. Although Harland and Wolff were best known for building liners, Belfast had the advantage of being on the other side of the Irish Sea and being used to building large ships. The Admiralty hoped that the H&W yards could work in relative safety and prepare the *Majestic*.

One of the Admiralty board disagreed vehemently with this move and the idea that lay behind it. As Third Naval Lord and Controller of the Navy, Admiral Sir John Fisher was responsible for shipbuilding at the time, and disputed the logic of sending *Majestic* and her workers to Ulster. He thought the entire exercise was futile, as he quite correctly recognized that the arrival of attackers from beyond Earth made a mockery of geography. The next Cylinder could as easily crash to earth in Belfast, Portsmouth or 'any other blasted spot' and nothing in their Lordships' power could stop it. He was overruled, as the Sea Lords decided that 'Her Majesty and their Lordships consider … action is necessary, for the maintenance of morale within the Service and of the nation as a whole…' even if that action made little strategic sense.

Fisher, however, was all for using what naval forces were available to bombard the invaders as soon as they were near a coastline, and regardless of any other damage this would cause. This horrified the other Naval Lords, but Fisher was adamant: any sacrifice was worthwhile if the invaders were weakened or destroyed. In this he and Lord Roberts were eventually of one mind. Unless the Martians were destroyed root and branch there would be nothing left for Britain or humanity as a whole (later, Fisher did get the chance to put his idea into practice with HMS *Revenge*). His mind had always had a ruthless streak, but the war against the Martians gave him an underdog's view of facing an overwhelming force. Fisher took this lesson to heart and became absolutely convinced that his beloved navy should never, ever be in such a position again. It was a lesson he used in creating dreadnoughts, a class of super-battleships that made all other vessels obsolete. Bigger, stronger and utterly intimidating, they were, ever afterwards, pillars of Fisher's policy. He remained bitterly disappointed that the Martians' weapons remained beyond human understanding and could not be fitted aboard 'his' new battleships. Until his dying day Fisher remained convinced that if the Royal Navy had possessed Heat-Ray dreadnoughts the Germans would never have attempted an arms race with Britain in the 1900s, or been so eager to support Austria-Hungary in its Balkan adventures. Those matters lay in the future; in August 1895, the Sea Lords faced and accepted the bitter truth that the Royal Navy was not the most powerful force on the planet.

Then they got on with helping to save England.

THE MARTIANS

Before considering the Fighting Machines and their weaponry, it is worth spending time on the Martians themselves.

To human eyes the Martians were hideous in appearance, the stuff of nightmares: rotund sacs of brains with hideous, gargoyle faces and huge, unearthly, luminous eyes! They were demon-skulls on octopus-like tentacles, touching everything with inquisitive, boneless, fleshy tendrils! It was an outward appearance that could have been calculated to cause terror and revulsion in humans. Of course, it was also a form that had allowed the Martians to thrive on their home planet.

After the invasion was over, some alienists, psychologists and religious figures claimed that the deep-seated horror and visceral fear felt towards the Martians were not only the result of appearances. They believed that these feelings were an echo of a deep-seated racial memory seared into the collective unconscious of humans. In short, it was argued, by Carl Jung among others, that this was not the Martians' first visit to Earth: human souls, collectively or individually, remembered the terror of previous encounters, even if waking minds did not. Such speculations were dismissed by researchers more interested in the tangible facts. Yet it remains the case that there was something uncanny about the Martians that made humans uneasy, even afraid. Veteran soldiers who were unbothered by ordinary enemies, men hardened by experience, were uneasy when guarding Martian wreckage during the rebuilding, even though everything was completely inert at that point.

Human scientists had few chances to study the Martians during the Invasion. They were hampered by the dangers of getting too close to the Martians, and by the military, who did not want 'tinkers, meddlers and bumbling crackpots' wandering about. Researchers were forced to rely mainly on second-hand sources, such as newspaper reports and eyewitness accounts of the Martians, although a few brave souls did seek out first-hand information. The Royal Society acted as a clearing house for what was discovered, and members put themselves fully, and patriotically, at the disposal of Cambridge and Roberts for the duration. Many were slain. No one who approached the Martians openly in the hopes of making peaceful and civilized contact survived the experience. The remains of the Royal Society's Welcoming Committee, for example, were discovered in a shallow grave at Horsell Common. They were identified only through their effects; their bodies had been ill-used, and fed upon by carrion birds. Like the many anonymous corpses found at all the Martians' landing sites, the Committee were cremated to forestall any possible pestilence. To meet the Martians, it seemed, was to meet Death.

As a result of these dangers, all serious studies of the Martians took place only after the Invasion. No Martian was taken captive by humans, so fate was a good deal kinder to them than to human prisoners of war. The Martian dead were in a poor state by the time investigations were begun thanks to three factors. Firstly, carrion birds and rats took their share. Secondly, the Martians that didn't fill crows' gizzards started to liquefy in very short order; extremely fast decomposition set in thanks, no doubt, to Earth's oxygen-rich atmosphere and diversity of micro-organisms. Thirdly, investigators preserved the remains in their usual fashion, with embalming fluids such as alcohol and formaldehyde. These methods were not kind to Martian corpses. Only one man had the wit to preserve Martian tissues by a different method: freezing. When news of the Martian defeat came,

Despite superficial appearances, the Martians were not all identical. Autopsies after the Invasion showed that the Martians had a malleable body plan quite unlike that of humans; even their internal organs varied, as did the frightfulness (to human eyes) of their external appearance. It appeared that they could grow limbs, organs and even teeth as needed for a particular task or effect. All the Martian corpses found within Handling Machines, for example, possessed extra manipulator limbs compared to the pilots of Fighting Machines. The bipedal servitor creatures found aboard the cylinders and in the Martian landing camps appear to have been no more than field rations for their Martian overlords. No tools or weapons were ever found near their corpses, and Martian machinery did not have controls arranged to suit their body plan. They were not used as 'foot soldiers' by the Martians either, even though infantry would have been useful in winkling out defenders in cities. Earth scientists are still debating whether or not the Red Weed was an accidental transfer from Mars or some kind of biological weapon. It rapidly covered the ground like a horrible infestation of brambles, and choked many rivers and watercourses in Southern England for many weeks, but seemed unable to cope with brackish or salty water. It spread up the Thames as far as Oxford, causing a minor panic among the evacuated British government ministers when it arrived. Sheep and cattle that ate it fell ill, but insects and lower creatures found its repulsive tendrils delicious. Eventually the Weed succumbed to earthly blights and only a few specimens remain in the collection at Kew, carefully isolated from contact with terrestrial species.

Professor William Rutherford of Edinburgh University had the good sense to telegraph a former student, George Challenger: 'Proceed Horsell Common and other locales. Preserve Martian remains with cardice [dry ice, solid carbon dioxide]. Will arrive soon.' It is only thanks to his original thinking that the 'exo-biologists' had any Martian samples at all, and even those were not of the highest quality. Challenger managed to freeze what remained of three Martians.

When Martians' partial remains were dissected scientists were intrigued and then puzzled by their discoveries. As far as possible, every Martian remnant was examined, and what was found led to some odd, even macabre, conclusions. Rutherford and Challenger were at the forefront of these studies.

To start with, some superficial features of Martian anatomy were considered to be bird-like. The skin was certainly as unpleasant to the touch as 'a plucked pheasant, hung for far too long to mature'. Martian bones were very light but strong, and included chambers that appeared to be connected to the breathing sac, something that was attributed to the thinness of the Martians' home atmosphere. That, however, was as far as the comfortable similarities went. The tentacles had bones only at their roots, with a fleshy lattice of muscles that could be locked together for rigidity when needed.

A Martian resembled nothing more than brain, below which there was an atrophied thorax surrounded by a number of tentacles. Most Martians had six tentacles, with at least two of these splitting at the end into smaller grasping 'fingers' for use as feelers or hands. There were exceptions to this, and corpses were discovered with as few as four tentacles and as many as nine. Even where the crows had not feasted, there was no pattern to the number of finger-feelers that any individual Martian might possess. Some feeler-tentacles ended with two fingers, others had as many as six. There was no reason to suppose that these fingers, of whatever number, were less dextrous than human hands.

All Martians had two eyes and stereoscopic vision at least as good as human sight and probably a great deal better. The eyes were much bigger than a human's, and had a crystalline outer shell. The size was an adaptation to the lower light levels of Mars, although there was the possibility that the Martians were natural cave dwellers or nocturnal. The eye-shell provided protection against the harsh Martian atmosphere. By comparison, the mouth was rudimentary with some individuals having bony ridges while others sported hideous fangs but no tongue, and did not appear to be much more than an opening into a gullet but without a recognizable digestive tract. There was a complex of airway valves and pipes, which explained how the Martians produced their musical hooting calls. This certainly explained the fearsome, ululating war cries of the War Machines.

It was possible to estimate the functions of some Martian organs: the Martians' internal gills were obviously respiratory as were the air-sacs inside their bones, and a large fluid pump situated nearby was identified as a heart with some kidney and liver functions as well. What was surprising was that no two Martians were the same when examined: the corpses did not have a uniform body plan for their organs.

Eventually it was realized that all Martians grew around the main gill sac, heart pump and filter complex, and brain stem. All other organs, including the tentacles, had 'budded' off this central assembly. They did not possess any kind of identifiable digestive tract; the Martians appeared to rely entirely on intravenous feeding. Around half the Martian corpses examined had what was dubbed a 'proboscis' in the roof of the mouth (for want of a better term) for extracting blood and nutrients from other creatures. The corpses lacking this structure always had a complicated pipework mechanism found near the bodies, an entirely artificial method of feeding. This method of eating was undoubtedly efficient from the Martians' point of view, but made them little better than blood-sucking ticks in the eyes of their human enemies. It also rendered them vulnerable to all manner of blood-borne diseases, which had been with mankind for untold millennia. The Martians were, perhaps, fortunate to invade a temperate zone rather than the Tropics, where fatal diseases were rife. On the other hand, they were unlucky to land close to London. While the city was undoubtedly cleaner than it had been, thanks to Bazalgette's vast sewer system, it was still a haven for many serious infections including cholera, typhus and tuberculosis, not to mention incurable and fatal (at the time) sexually transmitted diseases, such as syphilis.

The Martians had only the organs they needed for survival and to carry out their work. The dead pilots found in Handling Machines had more feelers than the pilots of War Machines, while those few Martians who had been found within the Cylinders had new limbs growing to suit their intended missions on Earth. Martians were differentiated by task, with physically different individuals having different duties. It was not possible to identify which, if any, Martians had been in command of their expeditionary forces based on their physical appearance.

As far as the investigators could determine, exactly the right numbers of Martians were budding new limbs for the positions that needed to be filled. It was not a great leap to propose that the Martians had conscious control over their physical forms, and could change their body plans at will. This explained why growing limbs had a great many more nerve connections from the brain stem than active, full-grown limbs. Martians could grow limbs and organs by thinking about them. The Martian brain was heavy and complex, outweighing the human brain many times over. This implied that the Martians were far more advanced in terms of brain capacities than had been suspected during the Invasion. It was also considered possible that the Martians were growing teeth to make themselves look more ferocious to their enemies.

The more adventuresome thinkers among the investigators speculated that the Martians might be telepathic, able to communicate instantly with each other by the power of thought alone. This possibility was elegantly demonstrated using two Martian brains within a 'Faraday cage'. By electrically stimulating a lobe of one dead Martian's brain, a faint electrical echo was generated in the corresponding lobe of the second dead Martian's brain, even though the two bodies were not in physical contact. This was considered to be sufficient proof that Martian mentalities were linked in some fashion, and that they could probably have communicated fully had both subjects been alive. Being able to know another Martian's thoughts in the heat of battle would have been a tremendous advantage. A Martian only had to think to have a message understood; the British passed messages by runners and gallopers, or by using semaphore and telegraph. No estimate as to the range of Martian telepathy was ever made, but it was felt that all the landing sites on Earth were in communication with each other. It was not considered fanciful that the Martians might also have reached their fellows on Mars by telepathy.

One worry about the Martians' mental powers caused disquiet: could they hear human thoughts? There was no proof that the Martians were able to sense human minds or understand them if they could. This was shown by the fact that humans had managed to surprise and confound the Martians in battle. This would not have been possible if the Martians were able to read human minds. They would have been entirely forewarned of all human actions. It seems likely that the Martians were in mental control of their humanoid servitors, possibly through an artificial mechanism. Many of the servitor corpses showed signs of brain tampering, and some had strange lace-like wires inside their skulls.

One other aspect of the Martians' anatomy caused some amazement. One corpse showed signs of 'pregnancy', with a Martian infant growing inside it.

Given that no sexual organs were ever identified it was assumed that these children, or scions, of the Martians were identical to their parents. However, the future parent and baby were poorly preserved, making a comparison impossible. No birth canal was ever identified, leaving scientists puzzled as to whether Martians were egg-laying or gave birth to live young. This gave the writers of speculative fiction a chance to invent all kinds of lurid notions, such as the Martian newborns bursting from their dying parents, or even very slowly chewing their way out (a fiction conveniently ignoring some Martians' lack of teeth). Later investigators have concluded that a birth sac simply dropped off a parent when the scion was ready to be 'born', with no more drama than a seed pod falling from a tree. Live young, though, implied colonization as well as conquest.

As far as anyone could tell, the Martians were a unified military and colonization force during the Invasion, and did not need separate formations or units for specific missions. The 'basic unit' was the individual Martian, controlling a Fighting or Handling Machine. Each Cylinder carried eight Fighting and Handling Machines, along with a full complement of Martians to crew them. Judging from the number of corpses recovered, they were operating some kind of watch or 'shift' system involving four operators per machine. This may explain why the Martians' machines never appeared to stop: every six hours or so a new operator could take over and carry on. This practice implies superb engineering and reliability for the machines. The Martians didn't allow for regular maintenance during the Invasion, and only repaired battle damage.

THE MARTIAN SERVITORS

A second species was found in the Martian Cylinders and buried at the landing sites. These grotesque, spindly 'servitors' or 'thralls' of the Martians were humanoid in appearance, although taller than humans. Given that very little Martian machinery was adapted for use by the servitors' hands, 'servitor' was possibly not the right term to use. Even as the servitors' purpose in the Martians' plans became clear, investigators shied away from terms like 'food creatures', 'resources' or even 'cattle'. The servitors were too disturbingly human to be comfortably classed alongside farm animals as nourishing meals.

On examination, the servitors were found to be distinctly primate in anatomy. Scientists had no trouble in identifying all the internal organs, which were entirely analogous to those of earthly creatures. As might be expected the lungs were of prodigious complexity and size, something attributed to the thin air of Mars. The servitors' eyes were also large and appeared to be very sensitive. This was also considered to be an adaptation to their home world's conditions. All the servitors had undergone exactly the same brain surgery or modification before they died, as far as could be told from their remains. Holes had been drilled into every skull at the temples,

and in some cases these holes were in the process of healing. While the brains were usually too rotted to allow exact analysis of what had been done, the creatures had apparently been lobotomized. In some of the servitors, elaborate metal lacework was found within the skulls, apparently wrapped around and through the brain. When three human corpses were discovered at the Brookwood site with head wounds and similar wires laced inside their skulls, there was horrified (but probably accurate) speculation that this was a mechanism for mind control.

It was obvious that the servitors had not died in battle; a few had been wounded by artillery shells and then treated. All of them had been drained of blood as they died. Thanks to eyewitness accounts, it was known that these creatures had been food for the Martians: rations brought from Mars to sustain the invaders before they started to 'live off the land'. The Martians either sucked or transfused the lifeblood of their servitors directly into their own veins. Given the remarkable similarity in anatomy between the servitors and primates, it is likely that these creatures were primates, kidnapped long ago from Earth. Once there, selective breeding made them a species of compliant humanoid cattle for the Martians to exploit. This might also explain the Martians' certainty that they could take human blood as an intravenous foodstuff: they had a millennia-old taste for something very similar. Feeding from humans must have been partly to blame for their eventual destruction, simply because the Martians had no immunity to the Victorian wealth of human infections. Perhaps Martian arrogance also contributed to their downfall, a belief that they would conquer come what may, and that nothing could stand in their way.

OTHER MARTIAN LIFE: THE 'RED WEED'

The third species of Martian that arrived aboard the Cylinders was, of course, the 'Red Weed'. While most casual observers considered it a plant, it was more like a fast-growing fungus. Its hideous tendrils and intense vibrant colour certainly gave it an unearthly, unnatural appearance, and its growth rate made it look more 'alive' and purposeful than it really proved to be. In Earth's oxygen-rich atmosphere and water-rich environment, its spores were able to infect and then destroy most other plants and fungi. It grew extremely rapidly in the presence of fresh water, and could spread along the banks of a river, canal or drainage ditch at anything up to 10ft (3m) per hour in ideal conditions. Rainfall, in particular, seemed to send the Weed into a frenzy of growth, giving rise to the popular belief that the Weed was alive (which it was, but not in the sense that common folk feared) and had a malevolent intelligence all of its own (which it did not). Fortunately, the Red Weed did not grow on animal or human flesh.

It threw off spores very quickly on reaching maturity, usually within a day or so, and these were carried for great distances by the wind. There were reports of Red Weed colonies being found in Holland, northern Germany and Denmark during and shortly after the Invasion. Whenever and wherever these growths were spotted they were put to the torch by terrified locals and soldiers. The Red Weed tied down troops that might otherwise have been sent to England to 'help' against the Martians. It also reminded every European government that Earth was horribly vulnerable.

The Red Weed reached central London before the Martians themselves, and soon overran the parks, most private gardens and, to a limited extent, both banks of the Thames. The polluted state of the river actually stopped the Thames disappearing. Even though Joseph Bazalgette's immense sewer system, completed in the 1870s, kept the worst of London's waste out of the Thames, it was still foul and polluted by modern standards. The Weed, however, made its way upstream into cleaner water at its usual tremendous rate, swiftly choking off much of the Thames' flow. By 13 August, the Red Weed had moved along the Isis as far as Oxford and caused a panic in government circles. Local troops were diverted to attack the Weed with hastily contrived gas burners. The burners worked, but the threat to Oxford did not last long: the Weed started to die back within weeks of the Martians' demise. Like the Martians, it had no resistance to Earth diseases or, for that matter, insects. While cattle and sheep would not eat the Weed, insects had no trouble with this new food. For a while, it looked as if southern England was suffering a second invasion, this time of aphids. The tiny creatures swarmed and multiplied on the Red Weed, until colder weather killed off the tiny pests.

Salt and brackish water, as well as salt marshes, proved a sterling defence against the Red Weed. Rather wisely, plans to kill the Weed by spraying it with saline were rejected. The contamination would have made much farmland useless for years, and Lord Salisbury had conniptions at the very thought of 'socialist' monetary compensation for anyone outside a small group of influential landowners.

THE FIGHTING MACHINES

During and after the Invasion, 'Fighting Machine' and 'Martian' were synonymous for Britons. Few humans ever saw a Martian in the flesh and lived to tell the tale, so ordinary people came to regard the machines as the true invaders. Their towering presence made them a sight that, once seen, was never forgotten. The Fighting Machines show that the Martians, despite what their misguided human apologists claimed, never had peaceful intentions. These murderous devices were useful only for an invasion, not a trade mission or a pleasant diplomatic soiree.

Standing some 135ft (40m) high, Fighting Machines loomed over their human enemies, implacable metal giants that could strike down enemies with fire and poison. They were armoured to withstand human weapons (the

Fighting Machines were not invulnerable; they only looked and behaved that way), and fast: terribly, awfully, hideously fast. The machines could sprint at around 50mph (80km/h) over open ground, although obstacles like woodland and buildings reduced this speed. Other than railway locomotives, nothing human could travel at such speed. It took bravery and discipline to stand against such monsters and, by and large, the British Army stood its ground.

On top of the three legs perched a precarious-looking control cabin. Legs and cabin alike were constructed of an iridescent material with a metallic sheen. The few pieces that escaped government confiscation have a strange, hexagonal pattern within their surface, almost like skin or bark. They are also a ceramic-metal composite, although few collectors are willing to have their Martian memorabilia damaged for any analysis. Despite the lolloping gait of the tripod legs, the cabins were stabilized and entirely steady no matter what the machine did as a whole. A single viewing port at the front of the cabin gave the controlling Martian a view out and down onto his battlefield. This was a commanding view of the action, and certainly contributed to the Martians' easy early victories. They could quite clearly see everything that their opponents were doing. British troops had no conception that they needed to hide from the prying eyes of giants!

Beside the viewing port were the Machine's weapons, the Heat Ray and the Black Smoke generator, mounted in a turret for use against ground targets. The turret was designed in such a way that weapon elevation, particularly with the Heat Ray, was awkward. The weapon couldn't be raised more than a few degrees above horizontal, and the Machine had to 'lean' back on its rear leg for some shots. The Royal Engineers' observation balloons sent from Aldershot were, for example, not quite the death traps that their users supposed. More often than not, Martians shooting at high targets were hopelessly inaccurate. Below the cabin hung a cluster of metal tentacles; these were used to demolish buildings or carry a fallen War Machine from battle.

While the mechanism and physics of the Heat Ray were utterly baffling to those who faced it in 1895, we can now say with some certainty that it was an immensely powerful laser beam. Lasers are now used for many purposes from surgery (cutting and cauterizing flesh) through to cutting steel, measuring distances with tremendous accuracy, and carrying information. It was the destructive power of lasers that the Martians had harnessed for their weaponry. In fact, given that the ray itself was described as invisible, the Heat Ray was almost certainly a maser, 'microwave amplification by stimulated emission of radiation'. The physics behind both are almost identical, differing only in the wavelength of the electromagnetic radiation (light) produced, and lasers and masers can both 'cook' a target.

A laser or maser is, in theory, quite a simple device with no moving parts, but it is something that requires considerable technology to make. At its simplest, it consists of a 'pump' or light source to begin the process, a 'laser medium' (a substance to have energy 'pumped' into it), and a pair of reflective mirrors (one only partially reflective) to act as an optical resonator. Between the mirrors, the light waves bounce backwards and forwards until released in a single beam of incredibly energetic radiation. The laser medium determines the light wavelength produced, and the mirrors bounce this light back and forth, reinforcing the waves in the process. Eventually, the light waves pass through the partially reflective mirror as a beam, and so the Martians had a Heat Ray. All kinds of materials can be used as a laser medium, and we have no way of knowing exactly what the Martians used. Given their scientific knowledge and elegant engineering, it was something that was easily available and convenient.

Shots from the Heat Ray travelled at the speed of light. If a Martian could see a target, he could kill it. It was entirely a point-and-shoot weapon; the operator had no need to take into account ballistics, wind, weather or even the target's movements. The Heat Ray must also have had a variable output, given that it could kill a single individual or melt a hole through a battleship's plating.

Black Smoke was made of weaponized carbon, the basic building block of life. It was not 'smoke' at all, but an aerosol of powdered carbon nanotubes. Nanotubes are carbon atoms arranged into tube-like lattices; diamonds and graphite are carbon with different arrangements of atoms. And like diamonds, nanotubes have their uses. Potentially, they are very strong indeed and they are beginning to have uses in all kinds of engineering. But nanotubes cause health problems if not handled properly, and this was what made the Black Smoke deadly. The Smoke suffocated anyone who breathed it in, as it coated the lungs and prevented respiration. Most victims died quickly, killed as they gasped for air.

Very small quantities were deadly over a longer timescale. It is now known that nanotubes can be absorbed into the body, accumulating in the gel-like cytoplasm inside cells, so killing them off. On a larger scale nanotubes cause asbestosis-like symptoms, and even cancer, in people exposed to non-lethal amounts. No one thought about such health problems in 1895 but, looking at the Registrar General's weekly returns of deaths, southern England and the London area had a huge increase in deaths related to lung disease, influenza, TB, and other bronchial conditions in the decade after the Invasion, in those old enough to have been alive at the time. Winters were not harsher than in previous years, but more people died during them than had previously been the case. Many who lived through the Invasion also suffered from eye conditions in later years.

The Black Smoke also had one other effect: it was a good complement to the Heat Ray because it had excellent thermal conductivity. A coating of Black Smoke dust would make almost anything vulnerable to the Heat Ray. Finally, a War Machine could shoot out a stream of Black Smoke, rather like a (later) human flamethrower could shoot a jet of burning fuel at a target.

The British Army's standard 12-pounder field gun was a reliable and accurate weapon, but it required a cool-headed gunner to hit a War Machine. It proved suicidal to attempt a second or third shot against Heat Ray-armed Martians.

From the few notes that survive outside sealed government archives, the interior of the control cabin was intended to fit a single Martian pilot. Described as 'disturbingly small' by some, the compartment was only a little larger than a Martian pilot. Below the armoured hatch, there was a couch for the pilot, numerous levers for his many tentacles and a curious 'skull cap' with many cables emerging from it. What struck those who saw inside the cabins were three things. Firstly, there were no dials or gauges or any other kind of display to tell the driver how the machine was operating or if anything needed attention. Secondly, not a single control was labelled as to its function (although no one expected to be able to read Martian script). Apparently, the remarkable Martian brain allowed the pilot to memorize every control. Looking back, we can make an educated guess that there were head-up displays on the cabin portal, or that the Martian pilot had some kind of direct neural link to the War Machine. Neither of these ideas would have even occurred to a Victorian. They saw only a confusion of controls. Thirdly, the cabin was armoured, so the Martians were expecting resistance and valued their lives.

A modern observer, with the benefit of a hundred years of science fact and fiction, might have concluded that the War Machine was a suit of powered armour for its occupant rather than a vehicle. This exo-skeleton quality would have made the burden of Earth gravity more bearable to any Martian user.

Available records show that investigators were baffled by not finding a recognizable power source: there was no steam or internal combustion engine. There was a helpful clue that meant little at the time: most people who sat inside a War Machine got a case of sunburn. It faded after a few days, but could well be low-level radiation exposure. The Martian machines were probably nuclear powered, and may even have carried small fusion reactors. To any observer in 1895 such a thing would have been utterly mysterious.

Communications equipment was not found. Guglielmo Marconi was experimenting with wireless telegraphy when the Martians landed; his success lay a year in the future. Later, it was realized that there were no Martian wireless sets. This was taken as proof of Martian telepathy: the Martians didn't need radio.

THE HANDLING MACHINES

Unlike War Machines, Handling Machines were not designed for battle. The immensely strong Handling Machines stood on six legs (this gave them a greater stability when carrying heavy loads) and were around 80ft (25m) tall to the top of the operator's cabin. They were not quite as fast as War Machines, but were a good deal more capable when crossing broken ground such as rubble and scrubland. A War Machine could inflict mass destruction in seconds; a Handling Machine, on the other hand, made death feel very personal indeed.

The Handling Machines were used as a form of mobile crane and 'wearable workshop' by the Martians. They did not carry a Heat Ray, but had a large number of heavy-duty tentacles; accounts differ as to the number, but there were always at least five. The tentacles did everything from digging out Cylinders and creating defensive earthworks, to recovering and repairing Fighting Machines and hunting humans. The Handling Machine at the original Horsell Common site spent many hours creating a defensive embankment to protect the first Cylinder; at Westminster a Handling Machine carried away the wrecked War Machine from Parliament Square.

The Handling Machine's cross-country speed made it impossible for people on foot to escape once the Martian pilot wanted to capture them. A Handling Machine's tentacles meant that it could rip apart almost any structure to 'dig out' its prey if humans tried to hide. At least one Handling Machine had a large cage on its back for human prisoners. The Martians came to Earth prepared to capture humans rather than destroy us all on sight.

The Handling Machines did carry a means to neutralize the Black Smoke. On at least one occasion a Handling Machine sprayed 'steam' into a cloud of the Smoke, and turned it into a thick, cloying slime that clung onto everything. This slime was just as deadly to humans (indeed, all mammals) as the Smoke itself. However, it did clear the air very quickly, presumably so that Martians could see their victims.

The ratio of War Machines to Handling Machines was around 5 to 1, about what one might expect of the infantry-to-supporting-troops ratio in a human force. The Martians had definitely come for conquest, not to build…

THE CYLINDERS AND THE LAUNCH CANNON

The Martian Cylinders were the means by which the invasion force reached Earth. They resembled huge artillery shells, hollowed out to carry the Martians, their slaves and their equipment. Each was some 100ft (30m) in diameter (around 90ft (27m) internally, allowing for the heavily shielded wall) and some 260ft (80m) in length. The nose was a blunt cone, and the

The Martians were incredibly lucky in having a mountain like Olympus Mons on their home world, a planet with an escape velocity less than half that of Earth. Their Gun-Launcher system was built on the mountain's slopes, a vast piece of engineering, but one that was easily within Martian capabilities. The whole structure was a giant tube-like barrel many hundreds of miles in length, constructed on mountings to take maximum advantage of rising ground. Side combustion chambers were fired in sequence to propel the suspension pod cylinders towards Earth, and each reached escape velocity without too much stress on the occupants. The acceleration, muzzle velocity, and therefore the trajectory in space of each projectile could be fine-tuned by varying the propellant amounts and firing times of each combustion chamber. With the Martians' grasp of mathematics and ballistics, this allowed them to place their invasion forces onto any point on Earth. Once launched, however, the cylinders were set upon their courses and only slowed when they entered Earth's atmosphere and used an aero-braking manoeuvre to slow down sufficiently for a safe landing. There would be no return to Mars for any cylinder or its Martians until victory was achieved and a similar launcher had been constructed on Earth.

whole of the back end was a circular, screw-fitting hatch. Such a description does not do justice to a Cylinder's menacing bulk, or to the tremendous engineering skill that it represented.

It did not take long for scientists to work out that one or more giant guns on Mars had launched the Cylinders. A gun design that, suitably scaled up, could fire a projectile across interplanetary distances was already known. By 1895 engineers (including Frenchman Louis-Guillaume Perreaux, whose steam velocipede was a forerunner of the motorcycle) had already proposed guns with multiple firing chambers. These, ignited in turn, propelled a missile up a single barrel at tremendous speed. This explained the gas clouds that had been observed spurting from the planet months and weeks before the landings: these were the muzzle blasts. As was discovered later, Mars had a perfect platform for an interplanetary cannon: Olympus Mons. This mountain is so tall that it sticks out of the Martian atmosphere into space. Martian engineering could easily have created a barrel along its slopes. A launcher on Olympus Mons would have been hundreds of miles long, but with solid foundations for almost its entire length.

Equally impressive are the mathematical and practical skills needed to fire a Cylinder across at least 34 million miles (54 million km) and hit a small island on Earth. As if this wasn't enough the Martians chose exactly, to within half a mile (approximately 1km), where they wanted the Cylinders to land. The scattering of landing sites was not, as some claimed, random chance. The Martians dropped their troops on their expected battle lines. The second Cylinder landed in Woking near the Horsell Common landing; later ones were always further away, and the final arrivals were dropping into the centre of London. The Martians intended their later Cylinders to be battlefield reinforcements. This implies superb control over the launch and flight of each Cylinder, and immense confidence in their calculations.

The Cylinders used aero-braking when landing, each deploying an immense shield to slow the dive into Earth's atmosphere. Unlike a parachute which trails behind the braking vehicle, aero-braking relies on air resistance ahead of the speeding object to slow down. Heating by friction can be intense, and this alone explains the heat given off by Cylinders once they had crashed to Earth. It also explains the immense fiery trails that were seen in Earth's skies before the landings. Other than soot stains on the outside of the Cylinders, no trace of these aero-brakes was ever found. The Martians' mastery of carbon technology perhaps explains this, with their carbon fibre aero-brakes being consumed during braking.

Conditions inside would have been hellish for a human, as not one Cylinder had windows or any kind of logical 'up' or 'down'. Each cylinder had compartments for passengers and for storage, but these were not arranged in orderly decks as on a human vessel. Instead, each compartment was part of a hive, nest or maze within the internal space. Very little space was wasted and, although it would have driven a human to distraction with its seeming disorder, the Martians must have been happy with the arrangement. Most compartments were filled with a jelly-like substance to provide protection for passengers during the voyage. It is possible that the Martians were asleep, hibernating perhaps, for the entire trip. Each Cylinder also had cushioned bays for servitors, presumably brought to Earth as 'field rations' before humans could be taken captive.

In addition to its cargo of Martians and servitors, every Cylinder carried Fighting Machines and Handling Machines. There were also spare parts aboard, and compartments given over to Red Weed. In effect, each Cylinder carried a complete military and colonizing force for the Martians.

There were some omissions in what the Martians did bring to Earth. They did not bring any naval equipment. This seems a peculiar oversight considering that they were invading a planet with so much water. After the Martians reached the Thames Estuary, it was revealed that War Machines were amphibious. The Fighting and Handling Machines had no problems with fording quite deep rivers and walking out into estuary waters. Crossing the English Channel or the North Sea would have been a slow walk across the seabed, but presumably no more difficult than picking a path through forests on dry land. The depth of the Channel between Dover and Calais is some 150ft (45m) or so, which means that a War Machine would have been submerged for only part of the crossing. The rest of the world was at more risk than anyone thought from the Martians…

There were also rumours that the Martians had brought Flying Machines to Earth, but there were no credible eye-witness accounts during the Invasion. No wreckage of any flying contraption was ever found, and this counted for more than lunatics claiming to have seen giant metal birds. Given the thin Martian atmosphere, it is doubtful that the Martians ever developed flight, but with their superior intellects they should have realized that a flying machine could work in Earth's thicker atmosphere.

CHAPTER 3

15 DAYS IN AUGUST

'This is a very ghastly business, and there has never been its like before.'
– Part of a letter found on the body of an artilleryman, after the Battle of Chertsey

WHY ENGLAND?

The precise reasons for the choice of Martian Invasion site in southern England will never be known. However, astronomers, scientists and military men made educated guesses based on their studies of Mars, the Martians, and Martian actions after the landings.

Giovanni Schiaparelli, the talented Italian astronomer, had made remarkable observations of Mars in 1877, and identified features that he called 'canali', or 'channels' (this word was subsequently mistranslated into English as 'canals'). Signor Schiaparelli's remarkably straight 'canali' or markings began speculations about who, or what, could have made them. In the light of the Invasion, it is clear that the Martians were responsible for these immense, planet-spanning structures, but they have not maintained them. Since the Invasion the channels have completely disappeared from the surface of Mars, and no trace can be seen today from Earth or from orbit around Mars. Whether the channels were dismantled or covered by sandstorms is not known. They remain entirely mysterious.

So, if human science was capable of seeing features on a distant world, how much more could the Martians see? How much more would they have understood from their observations? Martian science was certainly ahead of its earth equivalent in many fields, including optics (as the Heat Ray demonstrated). The Martians looked at Earth in some detail to determine the conditions their invasion forces would meet, and drew upon many decades or even centuries of earlier observations. Their records would have shown rapid changes on Earth, and in its atmosphere: great cities had sprung up across Europe and smoke from humanity's blossoming industries had changed Earth's atmosphere. Inevitably, the Martians concentrated their telescopic reconnaissance on north-western Europe, where change was happening with the greatest rapidity. The industries and cities of Britain, northern France and Germany led Martian observers to conclude, quite rightly, that here was the centre of Earth's advanced productive capacity, and probably the heart of its civilization. Would it have occurred to the Martians that humanity was split into many hostile nations and tribes? Probably not: they must have been a single civilization to undertake the massive Invasion effort. Even if the Martians did understand Earth's structure of nations this would have reinforced their choice of invasion target. Any Martian generalissimo surely wanted to destroy his enemy's main power to resist as rapidly as possible.

From a Martian perspective the best place to invade was close to the centre of Earth's power. And that centre lay near the north-western part of the main landmass, on a small island just off its coast. Indeed, the largest human city on the planet (London) was on the small island. Regardless of the social structures of any Earth creatures, such a large city had significance to the whole planet. The potential blow to the Earth's defences of taking it was a tempting prospect. The main resistance would be gone, and a strong lodgement made in its place, secured by wide expanses of water.

It is possible that the Martians were capable of tracking the movement of ships at sea, even across such a gulf of space as between Earth and Mars. Such movements would have convinced them that their target, the centre of a web of smaller industrial cities, and served by 'primitive' transport systems

Within hours of the first battles at Horsell Common patriotic — and completely fictional — images were being published in newspapers. Brave Tommies driving the invaders back at bayonet point were properly patriotic. The reality of humans taking on Heat Rays was never revealed to the general public. More than one newspaper editor printed such images as fliers and posters to rally the nation.

like ships and railways, represented the heart and head of Earth. It therefore became the best target for the Invasion; if the Martians could destroy this central hive the rest, over-awed or demoralized, would cease to resist. The planet might well fall in short order.

But to land in the middle of such a metropolis was to court disaster. What was required for the invader's first wave was a lodgement close by, but not so close as to be immediately accessible by large Earth forces. And so, we can imagine, the Martian war cabinet looked at their aerial maps of southern England, and chose an open landing ground between London and the south coast. The marshier land to the north-east (in Essex and East Anglia) was a dangerous unknown to a species from a desert planet, while to land to the north or west meant placing forces between large built-up areas (London, Birmingham, Bristol and the northern English cities) where native resistance might be swiftly organized.

The gently rolling countryside to the south (Surrey and Sussex) presented few risks to the Martian landing craft, and was ample room to manoeuvre after landing. And by such a strange chain of reasoning (although mostly conjecture from our vantage point) alien intelligences made the name of Woking an unlikely byword for otherworldly terror and destruction.

Although Her Majesty's Government had no inkling at the time, the war for Earth began long before Saturday 3 August 1895. Within two weeks British supremacy would be shaken to its roots, and the Queen's ministers would contemplate the extinction not just of Britain and its Empire, but of all Mankind.

THE FIRST LANDING

Early on the morning of Saturday 3 August the people of Woking and the surrounding area were shaken at their breakfasts by a tremendous crash as the first Martian Cylinder landed on Horsell Common. Trees were knocked down, windows shattered, and pictures fell from walls. In nearby Woodham Road chimneys collapsed and one house lost its roof. Remarkably, nobody was killed. The locals gathered on the Common, drawn there by a column of smoke.

Constable Thomas Barber was ordered down from Woking police station to '...put a stop to any nonsense'. Barber organized a rope barrier, stamped out the small fires started by the Cylinder's arrival, and then retired to a nearby hostelry to steady his nerves.

His superiors had alerted Scotland Yard, who sent three detectives. One of these men was from the Metropolitan Police's secretive Special Branch, as all the officers' details are unrecorded. Although it was unlikely that the Cylinder was a Fenian plot, Special Branch took no chances. Lord Salisbury's newly elected government was set against Irish Home Rule; a cunning ruse by the Irish Republican Brotherhood was a better explanation than nonsense involving a Cylinder coming from Mars! After all, in 1881 Irish revolutionaries had commissioned a New York shipyard to build a submarine, the *Fenian Ram*, to attack British shipping. Dastardly plots could not be dismissed, and telegrams requesting military assistance were also sent.

The crowd was more interested in the ale, ginger beer and snacks being hawked than mindful of danger. In London the newspapers had rushed out early afternoon editions all speculating about the 'Horsell Crater' and the 'Woking Martians'. Others in London were also busy on the matter: the scientific worthies who turned up at Burlington House appointed themselves the 'Extra-Ordinary British and Imperial Inter-planetary Welcoming Committee of the Royal Society' and booked seats to Woking. At Horse Guards there was consternation at being asked for help. The Duke of Cambridge, not in the best of tempers at having his weekend disrupted, decided that the army would help after all. Units at Aldershot were to be ready to move without delay, a difficult task for an August weekend with many officers on leave.

By dusk, and with nothing happening, the crowds drifted home. The sound of hammering could be heard as repairs were made to nearby damaged houses. It was around midnight when Constable Barber heard noises from the crashed Cylinder and realized that something was happening: the end of the Cylinder was unscrewing.

Martian Reinforcements

Two more Cylinders landed on Sunday 4 August; one tore through a wooded area on the edge of Horsell Common. Many spectators were injured or killed; carts and horse omnibuses carried them to hospitals and nearby halls. The second landed at Bisley, crashing across the new target range of the National Rifle Association (not to be confused with the American NRA). There, fortunately, no one was hurt although the members present gave 'their' Cylinder a wide berth.

At Woking railway station the first soldiers were arriving. Men of the 2nd Battalion, East Lancashire Regiment, were marched smartly towards the Common. More troops followed, and three field artillery batteries unloaded in the goods yard and moved forward. The next trains brought the 2nd Battalion, South Wales Borderers and 1st Battalion, Wiltshire Regiment. All three battalions were undermanned, but there were now some 1,500 infantry and 18 quick-firing 12-pounder guns ready for use.

Meanwhile the first Cylinder had opened and its top had slid off. Despite the casualties caused by the second Cylinder, the Royal Society's Committee, fortified by a good breakfast, decided to make their overtures of peace and friendship. The entire Committee was last seen standing at the edge of the Horsell landing pit. After they had descended, there was utter silence. The Committee members were never seen alive again.

In London there was much confusion about what the new Cylinders could mean. One Cylinder might well be an exploratory expedition or bear diplomatic envoys, but three? Were these explorers or the start of something more? The Duke of Cambridge decided to take no chances, and sent Lord Roberts immediately. His orders were to assess the situation and take appropriate steps for 'the defence of the Empire'. He was specifically told his troops were not to shoot unless fired upon. Roberts asked for more men and set out immediately.

On the Common the soldiers had deployed in a rough circle around the first landing (a small detail watched the second Cylinder). Officers made little attempt to use the ground sensibly, or to seek cover. They were concerned to keep the crowd back rather than contain a threat from the open Cylinder. The artillery formed a grand battery with an excellent field of fire across the Common, but no orders were issued concerning defensive earthworks for the guns.

By mid-afternoon there were mechanical sounds coming from the first Cylinder.

Lord Roberts arrived and, after examining the Common for himself, set up his headquarters at Woking Town Hall. He ordered a few companies to retire to the trees in case to form a reserve. Cyclists carried his orders to the troops, and messages to the Post Office telegraph for London. He already knew that the 4th Hussars, 9th Lancers and 2nd Battalion, Norfolk Regiment were on their way. And so he settled down to await developments. He did not have long to wait.

As dusk fell, a War Machine rose up from the Cylinder. It paused for a second and then began firing on all the infantry drawn up around the crater area, turning many into human torches where they stood. By chance, Roberts was present and immediately ordered a terrific barrage from all the guns into the first landing site. It seems likely that at least one War Machine was severely damaged in this initial attack. This is conjecture based on the number of War Machines aboard later Cylinders because no more than five War Machines were ever seen around the first Horsell Common site. All the other landing sites had at least six Machines present.

The Martians nearly always piloted Fighting Machines or Handling Machines on Earth. It was rare indeed to see a Martian outside either of these cunning contraptions which must have acted as prosthetic supports to combat Earth gravity as much as battle machines to fight human soldiers. The Fighting Machine was a terrifying engine of destruction for enemies to face. The Heat Ray cannon would have been bad enough, but the Black Smoke projectors gave each one more destructive power than a British Army brigade of the time: whatever the Martian operator could see, he could wipe from existence. A Handling Machine could be used as a mobile crane, mechanical navvy, human hunter and transport all rolled into one. Some Handling Machines also carried Black Smoke generators. The cylinders lacked anything that resembled a ship's bridge or engine room, and they were completely automated. The Martian crew either slept during the voyage, or had limited duties that needed little movement around the vessel. There were many pod-like structures, filled with a repulsive organic slime, that were probably protective shelters for the Martians to occupy during periods of high-stress flight such as launch and landing. There were similar coffin-like cages for the Martian biped servitors, and cargo areas for the components needed to build Handling and Fighting Machines.

The Martians pulled back, and the firing died down as more ammunition was sent forward. Having 'contained' the Martians, a few men were sent forward to scout the situation. This was dangerous work and many were killed, picked off by Heat Rays.

Those who did report back told of six machines: five War Machines like the first and a sixth 'spider' (a Handling Machine). It was possible to identify these machines by their different scarring from the artillery bombardment; the Handling Machine was quickly given a scornful nickname by the observers. Although it was unarmoured, the troops considered it to be a coward, a weakling or 'too important to get its claws dirty'. It lurked behind the others in the pit and they named it 'Frenchie', then 'The General'. A War Machine given the disrespectful nickname 'Dirty Gertie' (thanks to heavy powder staining from nearby explosions) quickly came to be feared by the troops because 'it' (the pilot, really) was an exceptionally good shot. It even seemed to enjoy killing humans by burning off their heads.

By dawn the human losses were known. Some 75 officers and men had been killed by the Heat Ray, but there were no wounded. The troops were eager to get to grips with the Martians and pay them back for dead comrades. Lord Roberts, however, was worried. He'd seen enough to know that his men were outgunned.

THE BATTLE OF WOKING

Although it suited the London newspapers to call this day's actions a battle, in reality it was a one-sided massacre.

At around mid-morning, with a tremendous clamour of hoots and howls, five War Machines moved out onto Horsell Common and put everything to the torch. The only soldiers to survive the onslaught were those who ran immediately. Anyone who hesitated was cut down. The Lancashires, Borderers and Wiltshires ceased to exist in the space of a few minutes. In the confusion that followed this day and subsequent events, only 53 men out of more than 1,500 ever reported back to barracks in Aldershot. One of these was a runner who set off to find Lord Roberts.

The 4th Hussars were mustering at the Shah Jahan Mosque, ready to go forwards, and then the Martians made their move. As is described elsewhere, they died almost to a man. The 9th Lancers, somewhat further back, immediately charged forwards and were similarly slain by the Martians. They died honourably and bravely, but it was completely futile. For their part, the British unit commanders in the field did not seem to understand the nature of the enemy they were facing. There was an unspoken assumption that the Martians, for all their powerful weaponry, were an enemy who could be countered with conventional methods

The grand battery managed one more cannonade, and then the gunners were overrun by the Martians. The civilians who had watched the military

manoeuvres perished too. The entire 'Battle of Woking' lasted less than 20 minutes, and the Martians were entirely triumphant.

When the runner reached him, Lord Roberts was horrified by the reports and in almost total despair when he saw the survivors running. What was left of the British force was in full flight. As an artilleryman, he was no stranger to applying firepower to problems, but something about the way the Martians did so niggled at him.

He came to the conclusion that the Martians had no concept of fighting, something which might seem extremely odd given that they had brought machines from Mars to do nothing else. Nonetheless, Roberts had spotted that the Martians displayed no tactical skill in battle. They hardly needed skill: their only plan was to form up in line abreast and then walk forwards, cooking their enemies as they advanced. This was horribly effective given the Martians' advantages but, once he had realized how they operated, Roberts began to consider how to fight back and not just give the Martians a new set of targets to broil. Perhaps human ingenuity and cunning, honed over centuries of warfare, might be of more use than human courage and British pluck.

An artist's impression of the gallant 4th Hussars' charge across Horsell Common, published shortly after the battle. Reporting the hussars' fate was forbidden to maintain national morale; throughout the Invasion newspapers remained relentlessly positive and patriotic in their reports.

Woking Mosque was the oldest Islamic place of worship in Britain, and a distinctive landmark in the area. Damaged when the Martians attacked the 4th Hussars who had used it as a rallying point, it was rebuilt after the Invasion by public subscription. The pitifully few Hussars who were only wounded in the slaughter found some shelter within its walls.

Roberts found himself bundled aboard a train heading for London by his staff. He refused to leave Woking until the very last moment, waiting to pick up any stragglers. It almost cost him his life, as the last carriage in the train was set alight by a Heat Ray just as the train left. Back in London he immediately upset the Duke of Cambridge by his new-found willingness to be ungentlemanly and, quite frankly, un-British in his methods. Roberts' personal courage would never be in doubt for a second, but he had grasped that this was a war of extermination, and accepted the implications of such a war. Gentlemen would be among those who died in front of the Martians; victors would be the ones to stab them from behind. He was ready to be as underhanded as possible next time he faced the Martians.

The Martians did not pursue Roberts' train. Instead, they formed a cordon around the second Cylinder, waiting for their fellows to emerge.

THE BROOKWOOD LANDINGS

Both sides seemed to pause and take stock. The Martians, having proven their combat superiority over the natives, were only waiting for more Cylinders to land. The Bisley Martians had been busy, constructing an earthwork bank around their Cylinder and mounting patrols that cleared the surrounding area of all human life. Meanwhile, on the 6th, two more Cylinders crashed down, both within the relatively open areas of Brookwood Cemetery, opening many graves in the process. The Martian bridgehead was growing and, seen from a Martian perspective, the sites at Bisley, Brookwood and Horsell Common were perfectly positioned to be mutually supporting.

A paralysis overtook the government in London. The slaughter of the 4th Hussars at Woking was considered particularly awful, as so many officers from good families had died. As the few survivors of Woking gave their accounts, disbelief was replaced by sickened resignation. The first reports had been dismissed as hysterical nonsense, but it became clear that Lord Roberts was not exaggerating the threat.

Defeat was not unknown, but this was different. The one-sided destruction wreaked by the Martians was the kind of thing Britain's enemies were supposed to suffer. The new government dithered, and then took itself to Oxford. Salisbury's ministers made no provision for the evacuation of ordinary people in London. As it turned out, the ordinary people of London stood little chance of survival unless they had money and could afford a train out of town.

Even as the government moved, concerns were raised that Oxford wasn't far enough away. York, Manchester and Edinburgh were all suggested as alternatives and dismissed for various reasons involving distance and 'inconvenience'. As one anonymous wag put it, 'That would be the inconvenience of not being a pleasant stroll away from one's club, broker or a well-run disorderly house.' Oxford was the choice. One permanent secretary remarked, 'My old college has some rather fine claret in the cellars. Can the same be true of Manchester?'

Once cleared of staff and students everyone agreed that the colleges did make splendid ministry buildings. Many European ambassadors and diplomats decamped to Oxford as well: they were all given rooms in Somerville College, the young ladies in residence being packed off to 'home, comfort and safety' until the crisis passed. The German and French ambassadors immediately argued about who had been given the better accommodations.

Brookwood Cemetery had two railway stations: one for Church of England funerals and the other for non-conformists. Other faiths were not accommodated. By landing at Brookwood and breaking uncounted graves, the Martians were accidentally exposed to London's dead, in their tens of thousands, and every pestilence that had killed them.

Shortly after the initial landings Joseph Chamberlain, the colonial secretary and Unionist Liberal leader, argued strongly for a government-in-exile. His Cabinet colleagues thought he was attempting to make himself the 'prime minister beyond the seas'.

Other diplomats left London aboard Royal Navy steam launches that carried them to Chatham and then home aboard their own naval vessels. A colourful collection of military attaches appeared at Horse Guards, eager to be attached to British units so that they could 'observe' the fighting against the Martians. Cambridge's staff sent them, with suitable letters of introduction, to Lord Roberts' HQ or Aldershot.

None of this was reported in the British press, because it would have caused unnecessary concern. The British newspapers were put on notice that they should not comment on, or mock, anyone 'cutting and running'. There were worries that repositioning the government might be seen as a weakness to be exploited by 'provocateurs, nihilists and foreign troublemakers among the disaffected of the lower orders'. The government, the ruling elite and the wealthy were running away, but they didn't want anyone to know.

In Cabinet, Joseph Chamberlain, the leading Liberal Unionist and the new colonial secretary (and a man loathed by many), argued quite forcefully that a government-in-exile should be selected and sent to Canada. There it would be ready to take up the reins of Imperial power should the current administration be captured or killed. Unkind colleagues supposed that Colonial Secretary Chamberlain saw himself as the obvious 'colonial' prime minister, and were surprised that such an avowed patriot would suggest even the appearance of abandoning England. Chamberlain changed tack, and suggested Birmingham (with its heavy industries) as the 'Bastion of England'. Chamberlain had reason to think this was a good idea, as he had been Mayor of Birmingham and knew his city well. Cabinet colleagues interpreted this as Chamberlain positioning himself to be the 'Saviour of England' if (not 'when', a sign of deep pessimism after the first battles) the Invasion failed. The government was new, and Chamberlain's support of Lord Salisbury was based on political expediency, not loyalty or friendship. He was divisive and unpopular, but this was doing the man a disservice. He was patriotic and meant well. Salisbury took umbrage at the lack of British fighting spirit that 'unpatriotic and lily-livered' critics showed in assuming that the Martians might not be beaten. Although nothing was done at the time, later on more than one minister found that his promising prospects had melted away.

The Crown Jewels and important state artefacts such as the Parliamentary Maces and Great Seal of the Realm were moved to Oxford. Oddly, the great museums and galleries in London were simply locked and left in the care of a small number of brave curators. Officially it was claimed that these sites were in no danger from the 'obviously intelligent' Martian invaders. Looting was not considered a serious threat as long as the government's departure went unannounced. Quietly, however, a few ministers had particularly valuable pieces sent to their own country homes. Wealthy private collectors, tipped off by friends in government, moved their property out of London as fast as could be arranged. Predictably the railway companies, led by LNER and LNWR, raised shipping prices in response to this sudden demand. Great houses were shut up for the duration but, as it was August, many of the nobility and wealthy were already at their country homes. The news of the Martian arrival was no more than an item for after-dinner gossip. Those with sons in the army were a trifle worried but, as private diaries and journals recorded, mostly that '…the boy did not let down the family name … in this strange business.'

The middle and working classes were largely left to shift for themselves. People packed what they could and left London, heading into Essex and Kent to get away. One railway company, the London, Chatham and Dover Railway, hit on the idea of using special excursion trains (normally for seaside days out) to get people out of London. They would carry away any who could pay for a 'return' trip to Margate or Dover. What happened after that was not the LCDR's concern. Many were still unable to leave as the

The Metropolitan Police were ordered to remain in London and carry out their duties, even as the government took itself off to Oxford. The officers of A, B and C divisions, covering Westminster, Chelsea and Mayfair, carried out summary executions of 'looters' in defence of their areas. As the Martians approached many large houses were abandoned by their wealthy owners, and word of easy pickings spread quickly.

Martians approached, even as the other rail companies copied this simple, even brilliant, evacuation-for-profit scheme. The poor of London were abandoned to the mercies of the Martians. And by accident the government abandoned London to its disenfranchised poor. This was to have serious public order consequences.

Even as it happened the withdrawal to Oxford was largely pointless. More than one general and admiral recognized that there was no way of telling where the Martians would land. They could as easily invade Canada, Balmoral, or the Oxfordshire meadows along the River Isis. As was often the case such opinions were not welcome. To offer them, let alone act in response, was to admit that humans were no longer in charge of events on their own planet.

In the capital, the Metropolitan Police were quietly issued with guns. The men of H Division, long regarded as a hotbed of crime, also carried cutlasses. A large number of police had disappeared, having fled with their families. For the moment the streets of London were quiet, but the Martians were coming.

The Battle of Chertsey

All day on Wednesday the Martians continued a slow, steady advance towards London. They were methodically clearing each town and hamlet as they went, burning everything they could or using Black Smoke to kill any remaining humans. Refugees jammed the roads, spreading panic or dying as the Martians caught up with them. By now, the Woking and Bisley contingents of the Martians were operating together, and a few brave soldiers stayed behind to send back fragmentary reports by telegraph. Their work allowed the next two significant British actions of the war, at Byfleet and Chertsey. In both cases, Roberts used artillery to its full effect.

At Byfleet two batteries of artillery were positioned beyond the River Wey Navigation Canal near Byfleet Mill, protected on three sides by water. Against human enemies, this would have been a strong position but the canal offered no protection against War Machines. Their stride allowed them to ignore the thin ribbon of water, while their Heat Rays allowed them to strike down any visible enemy. Although the artillerymen didn't know it, they were in terrible danger.

When the War Machines appeared, the artillery held their fire and then, as H. G. Wells accurately reported, destroyed one machine outright. Twelve-pounder artillery shells struck the control cabin of the machine and smashed it to very small pieces. Shocked by this event, the other War Machines paused for a few seconds. The cheering artillerymen did something exceptionally foolish: they tried to fire another volley. Roberts admitted later that he should have ordered the men to run after the first success.

The seven-strong skirmish line of War Machines fired all their Heat Rays at the same time, sweeping across the two batteries. Not one crew managed a second shot. Only those with the sense to jump into the Wey Navigation

Map of London and the Home Counties, showing Woking, Brookwood Cemetery, Chertsey and Aldershot. London and the South East were a most unexpected battleground for the Victorian army, even though its major barracks were located at Aldershot. A conventional invasion of Britain was never considered a serious threat thanks to the overwhelming strength of the Royal Navy. An aerial attack, or one from space, never even merited military consideration.

stood a chance of living, and those who did so were terribly scalded. Two Martians carried the wreckage back towards their landing grounds. The rest continued their methodical destruction and extermination. One of the survivors reported seeing the strange Red Weed growing along the canal...

There was a second artillery position at Chertsey positioned with considerably more cunning. Ten guns were placed inside a row of terraced houses, manhandled into the front parlours, and set up to fire through the front windows, which had been left intact. Once loaded, the artillerymen were withdrawn towards London. Only one sergeant was left with each gun, a lonely and terrifying duty if ever there was one. Even before Byfleet, Lord Roberts and his staff had realized that they could afford to lose weapons but not trained men.

Again, the Martians advanced in line abreast, apparently intent on destroying every large building in the area. Once they were within range, the ten guns fired as one. It was as if the terrace houses had fired a Nelsonian broadside at the Martians. Two of the War Machines staggered away, damaged; one was seen to collapse with a broken leg shortly afterwards. The Martians gave voice to a terrible hooting as the artillerymen fled, under orders not to risk their lives. Fortunately none of the soldiers were killed by the Martians' hideous response. Immediately, the surviving Martians fired into the artillery-packed houses, which burst into flame. They then liberally doused every other house in the area with Black Smoke from their projectors. It was this that demonstrated that Black Smoke could be fired like water from a hose into a target building. Weeks later, the corpses of many hundreds of civilians, hiding in their own homes, were found. After this, it seemed the Martians had had enough. Three War Machines had been damaged. They formed a defensive circle, and didn't move for the rest of the day.

The British Army, meanwhile, had been moving troops out of Aldershot and sending them south by rail, along the coast and then north up the Brighton line. All train movement near the Martians was now too dangerous to be attempted, although Winston Churchill had not received that particular message...

HMS *REVENGE*

Over the next two days, the Brookwood Martians probed to the south and west, following the railway line. Finding little resistance, they did not indulge in wholesale destruction but instead took captives, using Fighting Machines to herd humans into the waiting tentacles of Handling Machines. The prisoners were caged at three Surrey landing sites, as food for the Martians.

The 2nd Battalion, the Bedfordshire Regiment, had been ordered to patrol towards Brookwood, and engage the Martians if possible. Instead their morale collapsed, and the Bedfordshires melted away. This reluctance to engage such a superior enemy was entirely well-founded, but 'Martian Funk' was becoming a problem. Sending men to fight was one thing, sending them to be roasted with no chance of reply was something else. The senior major in the battalion was later found dead at his own hand.

Two more Cylinders landed at Kew, and caused extensive damage to the surrounding area. One Cylinder slid through the gardens, destroying the greenhouses and plantations. The loss to botanic science was impossible to measure, but fortunately the specimens of *Triffidus celestus* in the confidential greenhouse did not escape or survive. Mankind did not need a second enemy at this point. Many nearby houses collapsed, leaving little standing for approximately 200 yards (180m) in any direction. The second Cylinder completed the destruction. The Martians were unharmed and seen outside the Cylinder some eight hours later. They lost little time in assembling their Fighting and Handling Machines and, forewarned by their fellows, mounted patrols around their new home.

In London's West End there was an uneasy atmosphere. Large groups of the poor were roaming around, although not yet looting. Armed police and soldiers waited for trouble. By Thursday night there was rioting in the East End. The dispossessed had nothing to lose, even with the Martian

HMS *Revenge*, a Royal Sovereign-class battleship, was run aground in the Thames on Admiral Fisher's orders and then used to shell Martian positions. Her guns had sufficient range to hit most of London if required. Her captain, Lord Charles Beresford, was patriotic enough to destroy London to save it.

threat. Shops and public houses were ransacked and then drink fuelled nastier, darker trouble. Immigrants, in particular the Chinese and Jewish communities, were attacked for 'being in league with the Martians'; this was a vicious excuse to justify old prejudices. In Limehouse, the Chinese sided with the police for protection; it was rumoured that 'The Lord of Strange Deaths' ordered all members of the tongs to defend their people. True or not, there was little trouble in the area and Jewish families took refuge there.

Meanwhile, most Thames traffic had been downstream, carrying refugees, but HMS *Revenge* worked her way upstream until she grounded near Greenwich. Jackie Fisher had ordered the vessel into London, as he had wanted to use her as a floating fortress against the wishes of the other Sea Lords.

HMS *Revenge* was one of the powerful Royal Sovereign-class battleships, as formidable a war machine as humans could make. She had been launched in 1892, and carried four 13½in (340mm) main guns, and 6in (150mm) secondary guns, 6-pounder and 3-pounders for close-in defence, along with torpedoes. Her thickest armour was 18in (450mm) of hardened plate.

No effort was made to get the poor away from the East End, although orders were issued to police districts allowing looters, 'socialists' and 'anarchists' to be shot on sight. Some working class and immigrant areas were thought to be a hotbed of foreign-inspired sedition, although despair, drink and desperation did more to cause trouble than any tub-thumping speeches.

Held in reserve at Portsmouth, *Revenge* was now a tool of Fisher's ruthless policies. Each of her main guns could throw a 1,250-pound (570kg) high-explosive shell over 12 nautical miles (22km). *Revenge* packed a tremendous punch, and to be sure that punch was thrown, Fisher replaced her captain with an officer he knew would have the guts to fire on his own capital city. He metaphorically held his nose and asked Lord Charles Beresford to do the job. There was bad blood between the two men (Beresford disliked Fisher for his lowly origins), and Beresford was a 'loose cannon' in many ways (he feuded bitterly with the Prince of Wales). Nevertheless, the Martians needed beating and Charlie Beresford was not a man to step away from a fight. He was the epitome of a 'John Bull', bluff, manly and courageous to a fault. And he had the grit to do absolutely anything to beat the Martians.

Hyde Park and Parliament Square

By now, the wealthy end of London was virtually empty. Those who could afford to run had done so, leaving property to be secured by servants. Many of them had fled too, having loyally locked their masters' houses up first.

On Saturday a Martian Cylinder landed in Hyde Park, and came to rest in the waters of the Serpentine. The Martians were unbothered when they emerged. It was a mark of confidence that the Martians had planned landings in central London. They had launched this Cylinder many weeks earlier and had known, even then, that the open space of Hyde Park would be near the battle! Even more impressively, Martian mathematics was capable of sending a Cylinder to Hyde Park, a target only 350 acres (1.42km2) in area. The Martians had to hit it after an interplanetary journey of millions of miles. This was marksmanship beyond anything human.

When Lord Roberts realized what the Martians were doing with their landings, and the horrid implication that their war plan was on schedule, he fell into a deep despair. For hours he was depressed and withdrawn. Fortunately, no major decisions were required of him. This was his own personal attack of 'Martian Funk', and it is a measure of the man that he pulled himself together and carried on. He would not have been human if he hadn't been scared of the Martians.

Meanwhile, one of the strangest actions of the war was fought on Sunday 12 August in West Norwood, to the south of London. Hiram Maxim, the father of the machine gun, had workshops there, although the business was

Although rejected by the British Army, three quick-firing 1-pounder 'pom-pom' guns were used in defence of the Maxim Nordenfelt factory by Maxim's workers. Two crews were killed by Black Smoke, but the last pom-pom apparently did enough damage to drive off the War Machine. The 'pom-pom' name was due to the distinctive sound the weapon made when fired.

not thriving in 1895. One of the Kew War Machines was sweeping the area when it came under fire from Maxim's workers using a 'pom-pom', a 1-pounder quick-firing prototype gun mounted on an artillery carriage. The pom-pom was a scaled-up version of Maxim's machine gun, firing a 1-pound explosive shell, accurate to a range of some 3,000 yards (2,700m). This was more than enough for Maxim's workers to 'have a go' at the War Machine. They must have startled the Martian or hit something vital, because it retreated as quickly as it could. They kept firing until it was out of range and then, not wishing to push their luck, the workers fled. Interestingly, no Martian War Machines were seen nearby again. This success for the pom-pom was enough to persuade the British Army to purchase 500 pieces after the war to rearm with sophisticated and powerful weapons.

At almost the same time, another Martian force reached central London, presumably looking to link up with their fellows in Hyde Park. The Cylinder in the Serpentine had been under steady fire from HMS *Revenge* but without any visible effect. Beresford, having sent observers to the top of St Paul's to report the fall of shot, was conserving ammunition for targets he could harm. His observers now reported that he had his targets.

The Martians had followed the banks of the Thames into London, laying waste to everything on either side. For political rather than military reasons, Roberts had been ordered to make a stand around the Palace of Westminster. The government (rightly) considered that it would be a fatal blow to the nation's prestige and morale if Westminster was lost without a fight. It was the arrival of the Martians that galvanized Roberts and got him back into action. He had plenty of troops on hand, as the remainder of the Aldershot garrison had arrived in central London. He lacked artillery, but hoped to make up for this by issuing his men with service packs stuffed with explosives. These were to be hurled at the Martians when the opportunity presented itself. Given the weight of the packs, this would obviously be a suicidal act.

The Coldstream and 2nd Grenadier Guards from Wellington Barracks were the first to open fire from their positions within the Palace of Westminster itself. Their fire did absolutely nothing to the Martians at all,

The destruction of Westminster, the 'Mother of Parliaments', was a tremendous blow to British morale and prestige. It is highly probable that the event meant nothing at all to the Martians who could not have known of the building's significance as they carried out the action. All the troops defending the palace were killed. The British defeat at Westminster sent shock waves through the government, the Empire, and the other Great Powers. When reports reached Berlin, for example, Kaiser Wilhelm II was simultaneously distressed for his grandmother Queen Victoria, and elated by the humiliation inflicted on British democracy by the Martians. In public Wilhelm proclaimed his sympathies for the British cause; in private he instructed his chancellor, Hohenlohe, and the Imperial General Staff to move against British colonies when opportunities arose. As for the British, the burning of Westminster was the signal to abandon London to the Martians. Any kind of conventional defence was at an end. The remaining troops in London were ordered to regroup in St Albans.

other than attract their attention. Fire from HMS *Revenge* did a little more harm, making the Martians scuttle forward once they were bracketed by shots (the Martians were learning about human abilities and tactics), and shaking two machines badly. They turned and fired into the Palace, setting fire to both the Commons and the Lords. The clock tower burst into flames, and collapsed. Big Ben – the bell – plunged downwards with a mournful clanging noise. For a moment, all the British stopped firing. The Martians' symbolic triumph – a symbolism only obvious to human onlookers – did not last long. While crossing Westminster Palace Green, one Fighting Machine stepped onto a weak spot in the ground. This was the line of the Underground tunnel below the Green, part of the District Line. The tunnel was only just below the surface, built using cut and cover, and its roof was not strong enough to support the Martian machine. The War Machine's leg plunged through the crust and into the tunnel below. The result was exactly the same as a horse stepping into a rabbit hole, and just as disastrous: the machine's leg twisted and snapped, and the control cabin pitched sideways to land in the tunnel with a terrible crash. It did not take long for a mass of infantry to rush forwards and pour rifle fire down onto the stricken Martian. This did no harm, but explosive packs finished the Martian off.

This setback was greeted by howls and hoots from the remaining War Machines. For want of a better term, they all went berserk, releasing clouds of Black Smoke, and sending jets of the filthy stuff into every large building they could see. Stunned by this reaction, those few Guards who still lived tried to run, and died as they fled. The rest of the troops around Westminster died in place, struck down by the Black Smoke. Roberts was saved by the quick thinking of his staff officers who got him away on horseback along the Thames Embankment. He was also lucky that the Martians changed tactics at this point and began the systematic gassing of London. Only those who ran immediately and headed away from the Thames survived the next few hours. From Westminster Abbey to the Tower, the northern shore of the Thames was turned into a morgue by the Black Smoke. Further away from the river, human looters were beginning a spree of robbery and violence that lasted for days.

HMS *Revenge* kept up a harassing fire on the Martians, but could not lay her guns fast enough to keep up with such relatively nimble targets. The Martians soon had a line of sight to *Revenge* and melted the bow off the ship. The tremendous heat set off explosions in her magazines and HMS *Revenge* ceased firing. There was no denying that London now had new masters. As darkness fell, so did another Cylinder, although its landing site was to remain a mystery for decades.

HMS *THUNDER CHILD*

The Martians pushed on past London, heading along the Thames towards the North Sea. Panicked refugees went before them, and many tens of thousands died as the War Machines advanced. The Martians now seemed intent upon wholesale murder.

We come now to the battle that the Martians definitely lost during the Invasion. The captain and crew of HMS *Thunder Child* won a pyrrhic victory but by this point any victory at all was welcome.

HMS *Thunder Child* was a 'torpedo ram', one of only three such vessels constructed for the Royal Navy. To modern eyes, the *Thunder Child* and her sisters look rather like submarines that haven't quite worked up the nerve to go under the water! The *Thunder Child* and her sister ships, HMS *Polyphemus* and HMS *Adventure*, were not a particularly successful design. The ships were built around five 14in (350mm) torpedo tubes and were a bulbous cylindrical shape. As well as the torpedoes (and a good supply of reloads) the class also had deck-mounted Nordenfelt guns and a reinforced bow ram. The Nordenfelts were 1in (25mm) calibre guns with four barrels; they weren't quite automatic weapons, but they fired a lot of shells in a short time. The ram was included as a weapon of last resort. With a designed top speed of just under 18 knots (33km/h) (and the *Thunder Child* never achieved that in all her service), it was going to be a brave or foolish captain who tried to ram an enemy. Launched in 1882, *Thunder Child* was the second in the class and starting to show her age.

HMS *Thunder Child* was, however, the ship that encountered and fought three Martian War Machines. Her captain, Commander Horatio Welles, had been ordered to protect the pleasure steamers that were collecting refugees from Southend piers and carrying them to 'safety' along the East Anglian coast. When the War Machines appeared, Welles showed no hesitation. He turned towards the Martians wading along the estuary and put on speed.

Lacking oceans on their home planet, the Martians had no understanding of the dangers posed by warships and, in particular, torpedoes. Welles was given every chance to conduct a textbook attack. Aiming straight for the leading machine, he fired a spread of torpedoes at it, and was good enough to blow one of its legs off. The Machine collapsed into the water and a large secondary explosion marked its end. With no time to withdraw Welles pressed home his attack on a second, nearby machine. Every Nordenfelt aboard was trained on the War Machine's cabin, and shortly thereafter the ram struck the second Machine, bringing it crashing down onto the *Thunder* Child's deck. In a matter of minutes Welles had done terrible slaughter on the enemy.

As his crew struggled to clear the dead War Machine off the forward deck and Welles altered course towards the third machine, his triumphant charge came to an end. The third Martian recovered its wits and fired its Heat Ray at almost point-blank range into the heart of the *Thunder Child*. The ship immediately began to list and, her bow being dragged beneath the waves by the weight of the second War Machine, she was obviously doomed. Welles ordered his men to abandon ship and some dived into the water just as

HMS *Thunder Child*, a torpedo ram launched in 1882, was one of two vessels in her class in the Royal Navy. In action in the Thames Estuary, Lieutenant-Commander George Welles and his crew managed to destroy two Martian War Machines while protecting an evacuation convoy on 13 August. As the Martians waded into the water, Welles drove his ship at best speed towards the War Machines, launching a spread of torpedoes as he did so. Meanwhile the deck guns of the *Thunder Child*, all 1in Nordenfelts, opened up as the range closed. By sheer luck, one of the torpedoes struck a War Machine in the leg, bringing it down into the estuary. As the two remaining Martians stood over their flailing comrade a second machine fell to the Nordenfelts' fire. Welles kept his course steady and, closing with no thought of danger, rammed the downed machines, destroying them utterly. In the same moment the *Thunder Child* was split apart by the beam of the last Martian's Heat Ray and was lost; the Martian destroyed *Thunder Child's* escape rafts as well.

the Heat Ray struck again. This time the vessel exploded and sank, taking the second Martian down too. The survivors from *Thunder Child* expected nothing but death, and to see the destruction of the Southend steamers; instead, there was a tremendous explosion near the last War Machine.

The guns on the artillery range at Shoeburyness had now been turned on the last Martian. This was enough to persuade it to scuttle off back towards London.

Although burned and scalded, five survivors from HMS *Thunder Child* were picked up and eventually recovered from their wounds. Salty seawater, immediately applied, was just about the best unintentional treatment that they could have had. The rest of the ship's company, including Welles, was lost. All five gave the same story: that Welles had been the hero of the affair and had closed with the enemy in a fashion that Nelson himself would have cheered. Eventually, Welles received a posthumous Victoria Cross, the only one awarded during the Invasion.

THE ARMY WITHDRAWS

By Tuesday morning it was obvious to all the foreign observers left alive that London was entirely lost to the Martians. The British government and Lord Roberts initially refused to accept that this was the case, although Roberts may have been less than honest with his political masters. He and his staff had not slept in days, and they were at a very low ebb. He had ordered every unit out of London, to rally around St Albans. He sent nothing into Essex or Kent, where most of the refugees had headed. He didn't want his troops near civilians because he didn't want to put civilians at risk.

Privately, he hoped that St Albans was far enough away from Martians to give his forces some time to regroup and recover a little. The troops from the London and Aldershot garrisons had been badly shaken by what they had seen, and by witnessing the effectiveness of Martian weaponry. Roberts was no longer entirely sure that he could trust his men to stand and fight. Publicly, or at least when dealing with the Cabinet from Oxford, he maintained that he was awaiting a chance to take back the city. Setbacks would, of course, soon be righted.

As the army quietly left, the rioters became the *de facto* rulers of London. This state of affairs, disastrous as it was for good order, did not last long. The Martians killed many who remained, regardless of social class.

The Royal Engineers' Attack at Blackheath

Wednesday 14 August saw the arrival of the final Cylinder at Blackheath, and for once the army moved quickly. Tons of explosives were brought up the Thames from Chatham and then carried up to the crash site from Greenwich. This was a heroic, Herculean effort by the Royal Engineers. The sappers packed as much explosive as they could around the Cylinder, even though it was still extremely hot. They used fire engines to pump water onto the charges. The idea was to detonate sufficient explosives to crack open the Cylinder, or kill the Martians inside by blast alone. The work was given added urgency as the Cylinder started unscrewing; the sappers knew they had little time before the end cap came off and the Martians emerged.

Then another problem arose: a Martian War Machine appeared in the distance, striding towards the crash site. The sappers set their fuses and fell back. The explosion, when it came, was tremendous: every building within two miles of Blackheath had its windows blown in. The War Machine gave vent to what all the human observers called a bellow of rage, and immediately charged towards the site. The sappers split up into small parties and ran for cover. Eventually every man involved went back to barracks, although it took days for everyone to return safely.

Not one Martian ever emerged alive from the Blackheath landing. The concussive effect of several tons of explosives seems to have killed them all. Later, Lord Roberts pointed out that this success was unlikely ever to be repeated. The Martians were adapting and countering new tactics after seeing them once.

The War Machine that charged to the rescue of its comrades spent many hours setting fire to everything in the area, and releasing Black Smoke. Whether it was mad with grief, anger or some alien emotion will never be known, but it was certainly utterly destructive and apparently uncaring about its own safety. Many buildings were reduced to rubble, and the Royal Observatory was a particular target for its anger. The wreck of HMS *Revenge* was targeted by a long squirting jet of Black Smoke. As was discovered later, the few who had survived on board *Revenge*, including Beresford, now died.

The End

By dawn on 17 August 1895, Lord Roberts and what remained of the British Army had every reason to think that they were beaten. London was on fire; the remaining police in the East End were under siege; the Red Weed had spread across every park, garden and open space in the city; and the Martians were roaming at will, destroying anything they wanted. Despite the success of the

Royal Engineers at Blackheath, Roberts in St Albans asked for permission to abandon the defence of London. His assessment of the conflict was stunningly honest and forthright. HMS *Revenge* had been destroyed days before, and he didn't see any point in open battle: his men would be slaughtered again.

He sent a letter proposing a plan that he admitted turned his stomach. His staff had suggested that it might be possible to poison the Martians. By this point, the aliens' feeding method was known, so it was proposed to leave people infected with fatal diseases where the Martians could capture them and then feast. The Martians would fall victim to human diseases. Consumptives and syphilitics were recommended as the most effective 'Trojan horses', but other diseases were not discounted. Roberts recognized that only a ruthless approach would save humanity, but felt that deliberately sacrificing the mortally ill was a repulsive, dishonourable act. His decision to propose rather than implement the plan shifted responsibility onto the Cabinet. They were considering a further withdrawal to Liverpool (and possibly overseas) when Roberts' letter arrived. The Royal Household at Balmoral had already been told to make ready to leave Britain.

In the end, the Cabinet did not offer up dying Britons as a hideous sacrifice to save the planet. Nature and accident did what humans hesitated to do, and the death of the Martians, when it came, was quick and complete. The destruction of the Martians was so quick that it seemed they died without warning. By afternoon there didn't seem to be a single alien left alive on Earth. Survivors from Horsell Common reported that one Martian died in the middle of feeding, its human 'meal' dying from blood loss shortly afterwards. Other Martians dropped dead as they went about their assorted duties. The Martians did not show any signs of distress, confusion or illness before they collapsed. And everywhere the War and Handling Machines simply ground to a halt, never to move again.

This raises a fascinating question: why did all the Martians die at the same time? If they were killed solely by the action of Earth's micro-organisms, then the Martians should have died in roughly the order in which they arrived on Earth and were exposed to infection. All diseases have an incubation period and therefore the first Martians to arrive on Earth should have been falling ill days before any later arrivals. They didn't. Moreover, the early arrivals didn't make physical contact with any of the later landing sites, so the Martians didn't cross-infect each other. Even more oddly, not all the Martians had 'eaten' by draining human blood, and so they had not all been exposed to human diseases. Yet all the Martians fell ill and died at the same time, to the minute, as near as can be judged. Cylinders had landed at Brookwood Cemetery, it was true, but only a few Martians were exposed to whatever pestilence lurked in the corpses. But the 'Brookwood Martians' didn't make contact with their fellows and were therefore unlikely to have passed on infections from the human dead.

It was suggested later that Martian telepathy played a part in their downfall, that it was a hideous weakness as well as a great strength. Had telepathic trauma caused still-healthy Martians to die in sympathy with their infected fellows? This morbid notion gave hope that further Martian invasions might be forestalled. Perhaps the death agonies of the Martian spearhead on Earth had been felt on Mars. If this had not killed the remaining Martians, it would have been a dire warning of the perils found on Earth. This idea gave hope as the British government rebuilt the army, examined what was left of the Martians, oversaw rebuilding and, above all, kept a wary eye on the heavens. Perhaps Earth's natural defences were strong enough to keep the planet safe. It was also a lesson on the perils of space travel for humans visiting other worlds, although only speculative writers and fantasists were thinking along those lines.

When it became clear that the Martians were dead, the Duke of Cambridge sent troops into London as fast as they could be moved. He organized 'flying columns' using cavalry and yeomanry regiments from East Anglia and the Midlands. Their orders were to act against human troublemakers rather than the Martians. The columns' commanding officers were quite clearly told that 'Nihilists, anarchists, socialists and any members of the lower classes who raised their hands against their betters…' were to be treated as being in league with the Martians. Exactly what should be done to people in league with the Martians was not made clear, left to the discretion of the man on the spot. It's probable that Cambridge did not originate this order; summary executions would damage the honour of 'his' army. Few officers from rural counties had many qualms about the shooting of 'looters' or Londoners in the name of re-establishing order (a young Douglas Haig refused the orders, and then somehow lost his place at Camberley Staff College). More objected to orders to shoot the packs of dogs that had run wild after being abandoned by their owners. It went against the grain to shoot dogs…

CHAPTER 4
SEPTEMBER 1895 AND AFTER

The end came so quickly that the British on the ground were flummoxed by the unexpected turn of events. London was burning as the Martians dropped dead. The fires needed fighting and, for once, the rain of the traditional British summer was welcome. The weather did most of the work in washing away the dust from the Martians' Black Smoke too.

There was much to do. And, to those who had been caught up in events, it seemed as though little help was immediately forthcoming from government or anywhere else. Insurers refused to pay, pointing out that damage by the Martians and their War Machines was war-related. While customers grumbled, there was little they could do when Lord Salisbury's government, true to its principles, refused to intervene. Many insurers also refused to pay out for damage done by the Red Weed, deeming this an Act of God. Insurers were helped in this by the damage done to City offices and the loss of many documents; unkind observers felt that this 'loss' was all too convenient, but the well-heeled 'names' at Lloyd's of London had no desire to see their money being paid out. The government also refused to get involved in 'minor and inconsequential losses' due to the Red Weed. However, it did set aside money from the Treasury to compensate farmers and landowners, using the argument that food production was necessary to the whole country, and not '…a matter of mere finance'. Quite how this excused the payments made for spoiled parklands and ornamental gardens at some stately homes was never made clear. This money, as most liberal commentators at the time noted, went to Tory and Unionist supporters.

Fortunately, there was help for the lower classes. Municipal benevolent funds were established first in Manchester by the Methodist Church and later across the industrial North and Midlands. All gave generous assistance to the many families that had lost their homes and businesses, and now found themselves without financial help.

With the Martians gone, the human dead now became a problem. The Black Smoke was '…a cruel weapon that might almost have been invented by landlords for clearing out ungrateful tenants while leaving investments intact.' In the poorer parts casualties from the Smoke were appalling. Until Cambridge's 'flying columns' pushed into London, there was simply no one alive who could do anything about all the bodies. It was a mammoth task, and many months passed before all the bodies were respectfully buried. However, clearing the dead was a necessary task to stop disease.

Reconstruction was an equally slow business. Property damage was total in places, and almost non-existent in others, depending on where the Martians had attacked and the prevailing winds. However, within a year damaged buildings were being demolished or repaired. A shortage of skilled tradesmen and unskilled labour in London didn't help. The Invasion had killed a disproportionate number of the working poor; those who remained could demand better wages, or move to better paid work. The reconstruction saw wages rise all across the country. The northern mill towns, the Welsh coalfields and even the Belfast and Glasgow shipyards had to pay to keep workers. Many moved south for higher pay.

The destruction wrought by the Martians and the rioters had another financial consequence. Many government tax records were destroyed, and it was considered as easy to create a new tax system as to reconstruct the old one. Her Majesty's Government needed money and quickly, and

When military forces reached the landing sites after the sudden death they found that the Martians had apparently dropped dead simultaneously and in 'mid-stride'. At Horsell, caged survivors had a couple of unpleasant days surrounded by rotting Martian corpses but at least they were alive to moan about the smell! As always, illustrators of the time added savage-looking teeth to make the Martians more horrific and malign.

everyone was to be taxed, even landowners and aristocrats who had largely avoided paying previously. Emergency legislation inadvertently created a fairer tax system.

Belatedly, Salisbury recognized and resented the attack on aristocratic wealth, but he did see a silver lining in heavier taxes. He had no intention of leaving the lower orders with the means to better themselves; the higher wages of surviving workers were taxed to pay for 'Imperial Defence'. By 1900 the tax system took from the middle and lower classes while maintaining a polite fiction that the rich were paying more than their share. Having weathered the Invasion and the subsequent economic problems, Salisbury remained in power at the next general election; a vote for anyone else was 'pro-Martian'.

The army was rebuilt, although for several years there was a great reliance on colonial troops to keep order and defend the Empire. The 'new' British Army was professional and armed with the latest weapons that British factories could make, including automatic machine guns, Maxim's pom-pom guns, flame projectors and portable mortars. Along with these new weapons came new attitudes. The Boers in South Africa were shocked to find that the British Army no longer behaved like gentlemen but fought with grim determination against the rebels, making every use of their technological advantages and offering little quarter. The British Army, scarred by its experiences, no longer believed in 'fair play' in war.

Before all that, though, there were tragedies to be uncovered. Every Martian camp had its share of human graves, but one group of the living was pitiable. Survivors were found living in the shadow of the Martian War Machines. These individuals had lived in sewers, tunnels and cellars, and had managed to thrive in a limited way. They emerged from their burrows only at night, and each was entirely convinced that he or she was the 'last human'. It was a terrible blow to discover that this was not the case, a shock as severe as the Martians' easy triumph.

Thirty of these troglodytes were found. Each had kept hidden by day, foraged for food at night, and lived underground. All were relatively well fed but unhinged, suffering from nervous exhaustion and a variety of unpleasant diseases caught during their time in the sewers. What disturbed everyone was the realization that this would have been the fate of humanity if the Martians had not perished: men reduced to living like rats in the ruins of human civilization.

At least two individuals, soldiers by their clothing, fled from their rescuers, terrified that other humans were servants of the 'victorious' Martians. These sad cases disappeared into London's sewer system, presumably to live out their remaining days in terror of rediscovery. Of the rest, 20 people were cared for in Effra Hall Asylum in Brixton; all were utterly convinced that they were captives of the Martians, awaiting torture, exsanguination and death. A public subscription raised enough money to keep them in comfort, but all of them eventually ended their own terror-filled lives. The remaining seven needed much kindness before they accepted that they were safe; some even felt able to give accounts of their adventures and sufferings. One, the self-styled 'Professor' James Moriarty, a minor criminal and con-man, made a good living in America lecturing about 'Life Under the Martian Heel'; his experiences were liberally enhanced to titillate and shock his audiences.

Wounded British pride was not easily mended. All offers of help from the other Great Powers were firmly, but politely, refused. The Empire was completely untouched by the Martians, and its wealth could be used to rebuild. British pride had taken enough of a battering and it was a source of satisfaction that 'Britain' (not 'England', notice, although all the damage had been suffered in English counties) did not have to go, cap-in-hand, to foreigners. Salisbury's new taxes helped.

There was another reason for keeping the whole business a British affair. Sir Frederick Richards, the First Sea Lord, and Field Marshal Garnet Wolseley, Cambridge's successor, persuaded Lord Salisbury that Great Britain alone should have Martian technology. The British had faced the Martians '…gallantly and alone, and we alone should be the beneficiaries of our victory…' namely, the only people to get their hands on Martian machinery. The Martian weapons were too dangerous to fall into foreign hands, friends or otherwise. As soon as it was clear the Martians were dead, foreign governments generously offered their scientists as 'co-researchers' into the Martians' mysteries. France, Germany and Russia hoped to buy wreckage: the proposals including basing and coaling rights for the Royal Navy in ports across the world and when this failed, whole colonies. Russia also offered to abandon its ambitions in Afghanistan and the Persian Gulf.

Salisbury's government remained unmoved. From the moment the war stopped, a veil of British official secrecy was thrown over the Martian machinery. Military attaches found themselves 'encouraged' to report to their ambassadors in Oxford rather than tour battlefields. The Powers would be told only what Her Majesty's Government considered was appropriate, when it was appropriate, and possibly not even then. The army's flying columns of regular cavalry and Yeomanry had secured the Martian wreckage to 'protect humanity from any lingering danger'. This included firing on anyone who took an interest in the wreckage, as more than one adventurous journalist discovered!

The flying columns re-established control, and nearly succeeded in keeping Martian machinery out of foreign hands. All the Fighting Machines and Handling Machines were taken into British custody. However, one Heat Ray went missing from the wreckage scattered across South London. For a while, there was the unwarranted and unfair suspicion that Hiram Maxim, the inventor of the machine gun (and at the time still an American citizen), had sent the Heat Ray to the United States. He was entirely innocent, and the weapon had gone east rather than west. It was in Berlin, being secretly studied by the 8th Department (the *Kriegsakademie*) of the *Großer Generalstab*, the German High Command. It eventually emerged that its transfer had been arranged by Basil Zaharoff, the most notorious arms dealer of his time and the business partner of Hiram Maxim. In 1895 Zaharoff was one of the richest men in Europe, and utterly unscrupulous about the arms he sold, how he won arms contracts, or the nature of his customers. Somehow, he had gained control of a Heat Ray in all the confusion and sold it to the Germans. Zaharoff, however, did not sell them a power source; not being a technical man he probably had no idea one was needed. The Germans gained very little from what was undoubtedly a hugely expensive deal. All of this only emerged after Zaharoff's death in 1936, and was denied by the German High Command. German engineers never understood the Heat Ray, much to the frustration of the Nazis and particularly the SS who, by 1945, were in charge of exotic weapons research.

After the collapse of Germany, this Heat Ray disappeared again in the confusion. It was rumoured to have been captured by the advancing Russians. Later reports indicated that a team under physicist Andrei Sakharov had finally got it working, and this may explain why he was not allowed to leave the Soviet Union in 1975 to collect his Nobel Prize. The

Giovanni Schiaparelli's discovery of the Martian 'canali' in 1877 should have served as a warning that mankind was not alone in the Solar System. In order to be visible from Earth the 'canals' were linear features as wide as the Great Lakes of North America. As such they were civil engineering projects that dwarfed any human industry. Since the invasion the canals have vanished from the Martian surface.

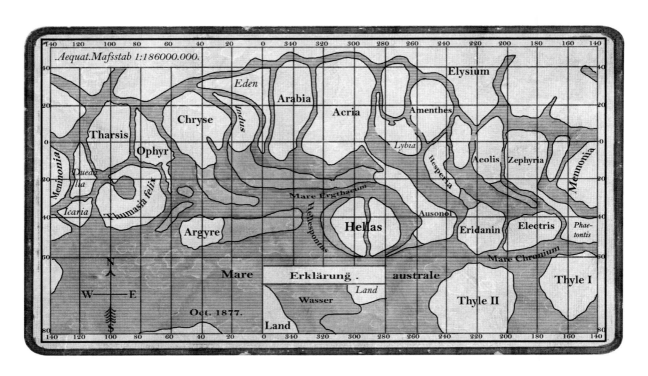

fate of this Heat Ray after the collapse of the Soviet Union is not known, but Sakharov's success does explain why the Politburo had confidence in the 'A-35 Anti-Ballistic Missile' system that protected Moscow. Zaharoff's theft in 1895 eventually cost the British taxpayer of the 1980s many millions on 'Chevaline', an improved Polaris ICBM warhead designed to get through Moscow's ABM (Heat Ray) defences.

Everything then, apart from Zaharoff's stolen weapon, was impounded. A tiny selection of Martian remains and artefacts were sent to the Science Museum in Kensington for display. One Martian was stuffed and given to a private collector. A suggestion that a War Machine should be used to make campaign medals was dismissed; there was a fear of alien contamination by the metal. Everything that could be removed was to be taken away. In the case of the Martian Cylinders this took some doing, and the Royal Engineers eventually used high explosives to smash the cylinders for removal.

The Martians' remarkable machinery disappeared behind a wall of government secrecy and official obfuscation. Within five years, even direct questions by MPs were being met with bland ministerial statements that divulging any information about Martians or 'ongoing scientific investigations' could prejudice national or planetary security. It is entirely possible that government ministers at the time did not really know what had happened to the Martians' remains and wreckage.

A hint of what had gone on emerged in 1955. Treasury documents released under the 50-year rule included an intriguing aside. In one (staggeringly boring) memo from 1905 there was a single reference '…ten years of work at Orford Ness on Ares-related materials … have yielded little in the way of results…' with a note that funding should be cut. The Treasury mandarin did not know or care about 'Ares-related material' or 'Orford Ness', but they were costing too much. Orford Ness is certainly a remote enough spot on the Suffolk coastline to be unknown to a civil servant in London. It was the home of radar research in the 1930s, and nuclear weapons detonator work in the 1950s. But in 1905, it did not exist (or should not have existed?) if official histories are to be believed. The use of 'Ares', the Greek name for the god Mars, as some kind of project codename suggests that something to do with Mars or Martians was going on. Maybe the Martian materials did end up in Orford Ness, protected by salt marshes inland and swift, treacherous tides offshore. This would explain how everything vanished so completely.

COULD THE MARTIANS HAVE WON?

The answer to this question is a most definite yes.

Even at the time, a Martian victory was thought to be only a matter of time. The heart of the British Empire was within days of being overwhelmed by the Martians, the population exterminated or caged. The British Army was in the process of being swept aside in the same fashion as Africans and Asians had been destroyed by European arms. And while Europeans had the advantage in their colonial wars, the difference between Martians and humans was a thousand times greater. There was, to be blunt, precious little hope for mankind. Wiping out humanity might have taken the Martians years of effort but, based on their conduct during the Invasion, extermination was their goal. The Martians were without mercy or consideration to the natives of Earth: they treated humans as cattle to be fed upon (at best) or rats to be poisoned (at worst).

In such a situation, would any kind of human resistance movement have been possible? Humans are nothing if not cunning and tenacious so someone would have fought on in the ruins. The locally-organized defence gangs in London's East End that assisted the police, and the small aristocratic group organized by Adam Llewellyn De Vere Adamant, give a hint as to what these resistance bands might have looked like, and what they might have achieved. Against a limited number of Martians, a few, disorganized defenders could have continued to do worthwhile damage but time would have been against them. The Martians were in the process of budding a new generation of warriors, and reinforcements from Mars would surely have added to their numbers. And then, as winter came on, the weather would have turned against any human resistance. The Martians, being used to the colder climate of Mars, would have been quite at home in an earthly winter. There would have been no pause in their campaigning season.

We cannot know how many Cylinders would have followed in subsequent waves of conquest, but the Martians showed a remorseless intelligence in all their efforts. Many more Cylinder flights must have been planned, if the initial landings had been successful. To judge from the Martians' choice of initial invasion site, their plan was to secure a foothold in the British Isles and await reinforcements from home. The war would have then continued against the rest of humanity. Realistically, their success could only have been delayed by human resistance, not stopped.

Even if the initial force was a one-off colonizing effort, expected to spawn new Martians on Earth rather than to receive reinforcement from home, the Martians could have constructed extra Fighting Machines from captured raw materials. Against increasingly numerous Martians, any human resistance would have had to use the tactics of the Spanish guerrillas of the Peninsular War: deceit, ambush and refusal to give battle on enemy terms. Such tactics against overwhelming strength can have disproportionately successful results. But they would never have been an easy thing for Victoria's officers and gentlemen, inculcated with the manly virtues of courage and fair play. Maybe, it would have become a patriotic duty to employ every underhanded tactic in the book to weaken the Martians in the hope of victory. It says much for the intelligence of young Second Lieutenant Churchill that he understood these necessities and possibilities, and acted ruthlessly during his escapade.

In the end, the micro-organisms that defeated the Martians turned out to be a better weapon than any battleship, howitzer or explosive. Sadly, this particular lesson of the war was not lost on governments, nor on the biologists and chemists in their pay. Humanity had been given fresh lessons in chemical warfare (the Black Smoke) and biological warfare (the fate of the Martians). Both of these ideas took hold in military minds and were used in entirely human conflicts, to the great shame of us all.

CHAPTER 5
LAST WORDS

THE 'LOST' CYLINDER OF KNIGHTSBRIDGE

The fate of the 'missing' Martian Cylinder remained a mystery until 1958 when workmen unearthed some metal fragments in Knightsbridge. The work was a planned extension to the London Underground station at Hobbs Lane where new platforms and an underground booking hall were needed.

At first, the wreckage was thought to be an unexploded German V2 but there was far too much material. When the Royal Engineers disposal team realized what they had really found, all further digging work in the area was handed over to a team from University College, London and the Ministry of Defence (to avoid inter-service rivalries). It took them weeks to uncover the shattered remains of the 'Lost Cylinder', and the decayed remains of its occupants. The cylinder had broken up on landing and had plunged deep into the London clay. The crater had then slumped in on itself, leaving little on the surface. By chance, one small internal compartment did survive intact, and in it were the skeletons of six Martian servitors. The scattered remains of at least 15 other servitors and Martians were also found in the wreckage, although little more than skull fragments and a few tentacle root bones had survived. All the flesh outside the compartment had been entirely consumed by micro-organisms, even in the near-anaerobic conditions of the crash site. There were, sadly, no new clues as to the Martians' purposes or technology: everything that was recovered had been seen during the post-Invasion investigations in 1895–97. Work was resumed on the Hobbs Lane Underground station.

Almost as soon as the station was finished plans were being made to close it; it was unpopular with staff and passengers alike because of the Martian connection. After 6 April 1967 trains sped past Hobbs Lane without stopping. For a short while it was used as a film set; Hobbs Lane was in good condition and there was the frisson of the Martians, although it was mostly used for (very) low-budget horror movies. Film companies that could afford better used the Aldwych branch line where a train was also made available by London Transport. Today, Hobbs Lane is no longer accessible from the surface, and any remaining Martians and their secrets lie in the London clay behind the tunnel linings.

The archaeologists never published any papers on the Hobbs Lane excavation, and University College 'misfiled' all the work at some point in the late 1960s, 'possibly as the result of an undergraduate prank'. The Ministry of Defence sealed all their files for a century.

Tunguska 1908

The Tunguska explosion of 1908 in Siberia in the distant east of the Russian Empire was huge, and its effects were measured as far away as London. It prompted the British government to offer the Russians any and all the help that they required to investigate what had happened. The British feared that the explosion could have been a Martian Cylinder exploding during a wrongly calculated entry into Earth's atmosphere. Well aware of what a second incursion could mean, the British made no secret of their worries in Moscow, and lobbied other European powers to mount an expedition. The British position was that someone should go and find out, preferably in force. They were, not to put too fine a point on the matter, scared. A Martian force in the wastes of Siberia would have plenty of time to establish a secure lodgement, and there was concern that the Russians didn't seem to be acting with urgency.

The Russians, not surprisingly, refused. Siberia was Russian, not British. The British minister in Moscow was called in to the Imperial Ministry of Foreign Affairs and given a severe dressing down for interfering in the Russian Empire's internal affairs. After all, Britain had refused all help during the Invasion and there was no proof that the event was anything to do with Martians. Several British nationals were arrested by members of the Okhrana (the Imperial secret police), and expelled from Russia for spreading panic. The Imperial government shut down all investigations into Tunguska. Not surprisingly, this worried the British government. Fortunately, whatever caused the Tunguska event, it was not a Martian attack.

Where are the Martians Now?

As the decades passed and the Martians did not come again we began to think that perhaps the threat was over. Maybe the Martians had realized that Earth was not an easy target for conquest. As human-built robots now insolently trundle across the surface of Mars, perhaps we shall wake the Martians. Or perhaps we shall discover a dead race, struck down by the psychic equivalent of a smallpox-riddled blanket…

APPENDIX 1
THE HUNTER

Martian bodies and artefacts were tightly controlled by the authorities after the Invasion. The only public place to see them was in the Martian Gallery at the Natural History Museum in South Kensington. This remained popular until it was destroyed during a Zeppelin raid. The only other place to see a dead Martian was in the collection of Colonel Sebastian Moran, the only man who was ever permitted to have a Martian stuffed and mounted as a game trophy.

Colonel Sebastian Moran, the author of *Heavy Game of the Western Himalayas* (1881) and other books on hunting, was a superlative shot. His military career with the 1st Bangalore Pioneers (Madras), however, came to a halt under somewhat mysterious circumstances; in August 1895 he was living in semi-retirement in London, his days spent at the gaming tables at various clubs, and in other pursuits.

A hunter during his younger days in India, in London he had a new weapon. Before the Martians invaded he had 'acquired' a Rigby .450 Nitro Express double rifle. Moran never explained why he needed such a powerful gun in London, a place where Bengal tigers were really quite rare. However, in the light of Moran's actions during the crisis the authorities simply put aside their questions. His achievement was enough to silence any critics for, as far as can be determined, Sebastian Moran was the only man to single-handedly stalk and destroy a Martian War Machine. After the Invasion, the directors of John Rigby & Company were amazed that Colonel Moran had even heard of, let alone owned, one of their experimental weapons.

Moran went after his prey by observing Martian behaviour from a distance over a couple of days. He was also fortunate in his choice of Kew, because it was a site where the Martians apparently felt safe. Always careful to remain hidden, he took no action until he was ready even though he witnessed the Martians' feeding process, something he later, and somewhat uncouthly, described as '… less conducive to the digestion than lunching with Scotch [sic] Presbyterians in a Limehouse brothel, and at their expense'. However, his meticulous reconnaissance paid off, when he spotted that as part of their regular routine the Martians always left one War Machine in the camp as a guard and reserve.

According to Moran's own account, he took up a firing position in the church nave at St Luke's in Kew before dawn on Saturday 10 August with a clear view of the camp across the rubble. The steeple, he later said, was too obvious a perch for any prudent shooter. He removed a section of stained glass from one of the windows and, being careful to keep his rifle within the building, took his aim. His exceptional marksmanship made sure that shots from both barrels hit their marks, even at long range.

OPPOSITE
Colonel Sebastian Moran (retired) was briefly feted as a hero for his single-handed assassination of a Martian. His biggest 'big game' trophy bagged, Moran did not wait to be discovered in the nave of St Luke's, Kew, and took to his heels. This was not considered the act of a gentleman. Moran remained unbothered by his critics until the day he died.

His first shot struck the guardian War Machine in the Heat Ray, which drooped and fired into the ground, starting a fire. The Machine was otherwise undamaged, but the Martian whirled round and looked in the direction of the shot, even though it must have been powerless to reply. Moran fired again, putting a .450 Nitro Express bullet through the machine's front viewing port and directly into the Martian's brain sac. The War Machine fell to its knees and was stilled, save for a crackling where the Heat Ray was still cooking the ground beneath it. It was the Rigby rifle that gave Moran's uncanny marksmanship such deadly effect. Compared to the army's standard .303 bullet, the .450 Nitro Express was huge: it weighed three times as much and delivered twice the energy into the target. Colonel Moran took note of the time and the target in his pocket game book and then made himself scarce, deliberately avoiding any other Martians.

After the Invasion he gave an accurate and convincing account, and his achievement was briefly feted by the newspapers. More was not made of it because Moran had only 'bagged' one Martian. A single individual, he confided later, was all he had wanted 'for the sport of it'. For him, a second Martian was no challenge, and so he simply didn't bother to hunt another. He wanted a trophy and with his stuffed Martian in his possession after the Invasion, Moran slipped back into the obscurity of his clubs and gambling dens, a most unlikely hero. The government, considering his unsavoury record in India and elsewhere, was happy to leave him to his obscurity.

WINSTON CHURCHILL'S MARTIAN WAR

One young man very keen to come to grips with the Martians was Winston Leonard Spencer Churchill, a keen young second lieutenant in the socially exclusive 4th Hussars in Aldershot. After the death of his father, the politician Lord Randolph Churchill, Winston's mother had used her influence to get him transferred to the Hussars. His father had refused to help with such an appointment because of the expense; some £300 per year on top of army pay of £120 was required to finance a junior officer's cavalry career. Such considerations didn't matter to the young Winston. Soldiering was his taste, and as a politician-in-waiting, he was eager to do well and gain a reputation.

In the 4th Hussars officers' mess the news of the Martians' arrival was first greeted with amused incredulity, and then with outraged patriotic annoyance: who were these Martians to make such an appearance, unannounced, and in England too? There was general agreement that the Martians were probably not gentlemen, were certainly ill-mannered, and probably required a good thrashing.

The 4th were ordered forward to Horsell Common on the Sunday after the Martians' arrival. Churchill and his fellow officers began to realize that the business was no laughing matter as his unit approached Woking. Refugees were already fleeing from the town, and the sky was darkened by smoke. The 4th pushed on and gathered around the Shah Jahan Mosque, a distinctive landmark just to the south of the railway line. The horses were rested and fed, and the men given permission to eat.

Then, with little warning, the battle found them.

The mosque's minaret was burned away, and within seconds the Hussars were destroyed as an organized force. Men and horses burst into flames as the Heat Ray did dreadful slaughter. Churchill was not burned, but was hit in the head by flying debris. When he came round the slaughter was over and night had fallen. Dead hussars littered the ground, the mosque was in ruins and everything stank of burnt meat. Churchill had been unconscious for many hours and, although convinced that even Aldershot lay in ruins, he made his way west along the railway line. In doing so he also stumbled right into the waiting tentacles of a Handling Machine and was captured.

He was taken to the second Martian camp, in Brookwood Cemetery, and witnessed the Martians feeding on their captives. A lesser man might well have gone mad at that moment, but Churchill had the strength of character

to convince his fellow prisoners that escape was still possible. He was also armed, as the Martians hadn't bothered taking his service revolver. He shot out the locking mechanism of the cage, but many escaping prisoners were cut down by Heat Rays. Churchill was among the lucky ones, and was able to hide among Brookwood's many tombs until night fell again.

Desperately tired and hungry, Churchill again followed the railway, this time heading towards London. Along the way he collected a band of stragglers from various units, 'waifs, strays and good honest fighting men, but all plucky fellows of the best English stock'. Beyond their own experiences, these men had no idea what was happening, but Churchill learned that the 4th Hussars no longer existed; he was the last surviving officer. On several occasions they had to hide from Martian patrols but the group reached Waterloo after three days, only to find it deserted.

It was there that one of the 'plucky fellows', Albert Perks, an experienced engine driver, spotted that there was an ordnance train sitting at one of the platforms. It was stuffed with explosives, and Churchill decided to take the train back to Brookwood to blow up the Martians there '...with all their blood-stained and alien filth'. Churchill had recognized that half-measures of any kind would not work against the Martians. Perks – an absolutely vital part of the scheme – was willing to drive the train. They contrived a series of slow fuses from the cab to the explosives, and set off. Everything went well, with Churchill leaping from the train to alter the points as needed.

They did not, however, get as far as Brookwood. Instead, at Weybridge station, they met a Martian War Machine walking along the line towards London. By Churchill's own account, he and Driver Perks set the fuses and accelerated towards the Martian. The Heat Ray struck the locomotive, causing the boiler to burst. Perks was killed instantaneously, Churchill was thrown clear and in the next moment the wrecked train rolled to a halt at the feet of the War Machine and its cargo exploded, removing all the Machine's legs in the explosion. Churchill had the presence of

Tales of heroism and 'manly British pluck' during the Invasion were thin on the ground, so Second Lieutenant Churchill's escape from the Martian encampment at Brookwood had all the elements of luck, pluck and derring-do that any patriot could have wanted. Churchill had been taken, while unconscious, to the Martians' camp. When he witnessed what the Martians were doing to captives, Churchill hurriedly organized a breakout by the military prisoners. While many were killed, Churchill managed to get away in the confusion and hide among the graves in Brookwood Cemetery. He followed the London and South Western Railway line (the Necropolis Railway trains to Brookwood used their track) back towards London only to find the city deserted. Collecting a ragtag group of soldiers, he took his revenge on the Brookwood Martians and then led his men on foot to Horse Guards. Several times they skirmished with bands of looters before reaching army headquarters, and then attached his rag-tag force to the Metropolitan Police. In the illustration Churchill carries his own .455 Webley revolver; he had another recovered from a fellow officer's corpse. By Churchill's own account, the Martians took all the rifles and swords from their captives but never bothered to search for smaller weapons. Churchill's escape turned out to be the first and last of its kind as Martian security improved. Survivors among those captured after Churchill's adventures reported that the Martians later made a point of removing anything that looked like a weapon from prisoners.

mind to pick up a fragment of Martian metal and run for his life. After this, Churchill returned to London and was attached to the Metropolitan Police; he spent his time as a liaison officer shooting looters in the West End before the Martians set fire to much of the city.

After the Invasion, Churchill's account of his destruction of a War Machine was accepted without challenge, and he was mentioned in dispatches. This ignored the probability that Churchill should have been killed if all had happened as he claimed. The country, however, needed heroes. Lady Jenny Churchill lobbied vigorously among her many friends and admirers for her son to be 'properly' rewarded for his gallantry in single-handedly destroying a Martian, but medals were thin on the ground for everyone. The efforts of the unfortunate Mr Perks were conveniently overlooked. Churchill was happy enough to be mentioned, as this gave him some credibility for his political ambitions and he did mention Mr Perks' part in his newspaper articles, an act of honesty that rather annoyed his ambitious mother.